Into the burning silence, he said persuasively, "Look, enough messing around. How about I put a serious deal on the table? Something that will meet your needs as well as my own."

They were standing very close, almost touching. The fragrant heat off her body was driving Rafael's senses crazy, his pulse racing, his mouth dry with longing.

"What kind of deal?" she asked suspiciously.

Did he dare make the offer he was so impulsively contemplating? It was off-the-charts outrageous. But hell, why not throw it out there and see what the reaction was? It would be the perfect solution to his current difficulties.

"Marry me."

"What... What did you say?" Sabrina seemed stunned by his husky command, as well she might be. It was a fantastical proposal, of course it was. And yet he meant it. Her lips parted as though sensing the seriousness of his intent, eyes widening, a confused, storm-tossed blue. "You must be mad."

"You want the orphanage. I'll sell it to you in exchange for..." He drew an unsteady breath, not quite believing he was actually saying it. "My wedding ring on your finger."

Jane Holland grew up in a house of writers. Her mother was bestselling Harlequin author Charlotte Lamb, her sister also penned romances and her father was a journalist and biographer. Small wonder she became a writer herself! Starting off in poetry, historical fiction and thrillers, she's now proud to be following in her mother's footsteps writing romance for Harlequin. A mum of five, she loves tramping the Cornish coast, and often writes with a cat on her lap.

This is Jane Holland's debut book for Harlequin Presents—we hope that you enjoy it!

Jane Holland

HER CONVENIENT VOW
TO THE BILLIONAIRE

HARLEQUIN®
PRESENTS™

Recycling programs for this product may not exist in your area.

ISBN-13: 978-1-335-59285-9

Her Convenient Vow to the Billionaire

For questions and comments about the quality of this book, please contact us at CustomerService@Harlequin.com.

Harlequin Enterprises ULC
22 Adelaide St. West, 41st Floor
Toronto, Ontario M5H 4E3, Canada
www.Harlequin.com

Printed in U.S.A.

HER CONVENIENT VOW
TO THE BILLIONAIRE

In memory of my mother, Charlotte Lamb, a much-beloved Harlequin author herself and an amazing woman. This one's for you, Mum!

CHAPTER ONE

'SABRINA,' BARKED THE voice on the other end of the phone, prompting an instinctive flush of guilt. 'What on earth are you doing back on Calista?'

It was the same question Sabrina had been secretly asking herself for the past twenty-four hours, couched now in her father's terse tones and delivered directly into her ear. Even though she had doubts about this return to the Greek island where she'd been born and raised, his peremptory demand prickled at her nerves. She wished he would trust her a little more, the way he trusted his other two children, Tom and Pippa. But they were his own flesh and blood, unlike her.

'Um…unfinished business.' Switching to speaker phone, she set her mobile on the stone step beside her. She needed to listen out for a vehicle approaching. 'It shouldn't take long, Dad, I promise.'

'What unfinished business? What are you talking about?'

Sabrina sat down in the shade of the old orphanage and began to smooth out the tangles in her wayward blonde hair. She'd forgotten how intense and unrelenting the heat could be on this tiny island. She'd hired a sports car on the mainland and brought it over on the ferry last night—the island was too small for a proper airfield—and driven here from her harbourside hotel this morning with the top down, wind in her hair. Now her ordinarily sleek hair more closely resembled a briar patch.

'Nothing important.' Stumbling over the little white lie, she winced. 'I'll tell you when I get home.'

'I'd rather you told me now...'

Her father's voice deepened, his sympathy triggering the anxious little girl still inside her.

'This is me, Sabrina. You don't have to pretend. I know you haven't been back to Calista since...' He stopped, abruptly changing tack. 'Look, just tell me what you're up to, darling. Let me be the judge of whether it's important or not.'

Sabrina rested her forehead on her hand, groaning inwardly. She loved him, this extraordinary billionaire who had rescued her from an ignominious existence, brought her into the heart of his family and allowed her to blossom into the high-flying executive she was today. She would always be grateful to him. But he couldn't keep interfering in her life. Even now she was heading towards her thirties, he still seemed to view her as a child.

'Sorry, Dad. You're... You're breaking up. Poor reception.' She rolled her eyes at this unlikely excuse, finishing apologetically, 'Call you back later, okay? Love you loads.'

Turning off her phone with a grimace, she stood up,

brushing dust off the white silk dress she'd chosen for this difficult meeting.

Andrew Richard Templeton, OBE, would be angry at her for terminating his call. She admitted to some trepidation at that thought, for she hated disappointing him by not acting the obedient daughter. But right now she couldn't deal with his mother hen approach to parenting. Not today. His well-intentioned desire to shield her from life's knocks would only sap her confidence, and she needed all her strength and focus for the negotiations to come.

Assuming anyone turned up to negotiate, that was...

Against the rhythmic *chi-chi-chi* of cicadas in the heat, Sabrina gazed up at the orphanage, tilting her head to take it all in.

The cracked, whitewashed walls had been softened since her time by fragrant ropes of bright, flowering bougainvillea that were gradually taking over the place. The sloping roof where she and her friends had sometimes crept out to sunbathe was missing a few terracotta tiles. As she descended the steps into the deep hollow where the orphanage nestled, a lizard with jewelled eyes blinked at her, and then zigzagged up the sun-baked wall to disappear behind a clump of brilliant magenta flowers.

The front entrance, a flaking blue door that sagged in its frame, stood closed. There was an official-looking notice nailed to the door. She scanned the warning, written in Greek, that stated the building was due to be demolished.

Tears flooded Sabrina's eyes and she struggled against

the urge to shout furious obscenities at the innocent air. Instead, she contented herself with a muffled sob. 'How dare he? I won't allow it.'

The painted sign above the door said, *Calista Orphanage*.

This was where they'd brought her as a terrified orphan, lost without her single parent mother, too scared to raise her head in case anyone saw her scar-ravaged face.

Yet, despite her fears, the orphanage had become her home, and since nobody had liked the look of her enough to adopt her until she was sixteen, this place had dug deep into her heart and refused to be dislodged.

Here, she'd run wild and free, lost herself in books and poetry, skinned her knees playing games of tag, and made the best friend in the whole world. As much as a girl could ever be friends with a tough young urchin with jet-black hair and fists permanently clenched for battle.

Trying the door, she found it unlocked. The orphanage stood several miles from the island's main port, deep in dusty, sun-drenched countryside. Nobody would come all the way out here to rob an empty building.

Sabrina wandered through familiar rooms long since emptied of their contents. Her high heels—unsuitable for the terrain, but providing much-needed extra inches for today's meeting—echoed on the worn stone flags. She paused in each doorway, hearing the ghosts of laughter and teenage chatter in her head, and even peered up the stairs into the honey-coloured gloom, half expecting to see Yannis or Melantha standing there.

Clenching her jaw, she felt abruptly furious again. She couldn't allow this place to be knocked down. Whatever the cost, it must be renovated instead. But she could already hear her father's calm, prosaic analysis. *A waste of money*, he would say, and he'd be right. But not everything was about the bottom line. Sometimes the heart needed to be reckoned with as well.

The choice was not hers to make, though. That was the difficulty.

Sabrina took a deep breath and let it out unsteadily. It was by the merest chance that she'd heard of the decision to demolish the former children's home. Nobody could have guessed, herself included, how vehemently she would react to the news.

Kind and generous though Andrew Templeton was, there had always been something missing from her relationship with her adoptive father. His fabulous wealth was no substitute for the close bond she'd enjoyed with her mother here on Calista. Perhaps that was why she still felt such emotion for this ramshackle old building with its homely rooms and cosy corners. Losing it would be like losing her mother all over again.

Peering into the small hall where they'd used to gather for performances or indoor sports, Sabrina froze, her head raised to listen.

Only it wasn't a car engine she heard.

Her heart began to thud.

It was a helicopter. Which meant only one thing.

Sabrina hurried up the stairs for a better vantage point. From his PA's email, sent three days ago, she'd assumed he would be sending a lackey to this meeting—some representative who would listen politely and report back to him.

No lackey would arrive in a helicopter.

Upstairs, sunlight struck through the dusty first-floor windows with a fierce glow. As a child, she'd had to stretch on full tiptoe to peer out of this window. Now she stood in imposing stilettos with a platinum heel and stared across the orphanage grounds to where a helicopter was majestically descending. Its rotor blades winnowed the leafy trees and shrubs, dragging up dust in an ever-growing spiral. His company logo was on the side panel, but the glass was tinted, making it impossible to see who was inside. Then the helicopter touched down and, while the blades were still spinning, the door was thrown open and a man jumped to the ground.

Sabrina gasped, her heart in freefall.

Both hands wide against the window, fingertips white with pressure, she thrust her face against the dirty glass to stare down at him, still unable to believe he had chosen to come to the orphanage himself.

Hadn't he realised she would be at this meeting? Or perhaps he had imagined she would be accompanied by a personal assistant or two. But she'd deliberately left her entourage behind for this trip, guarding her past even from the people who worked for her. Besides, she'd preferred the idea of walking about the orphanage alone beforehand, revisiting the sweetly scented haunts of her childhood home without being observed.

Now he was here too. And alone, just like her.

It had been five years since their disastrous last meeting, at a charity ball in Paris—the first time they'd seen each other since their teenage years. Sabrina had greeted her best friend with shy excitement, giddy to see him again, her heart thumping. She'd watched his meteoric rise in a business career with interest over the years but never quite dared contact him, knowing how bitter he'd felt when she'd been adopted at sixteen and left him behind. He had never replied to her letters, she'd thought, so why would he welcome her with open arms?

But then he'd hugged her in greeting and she'd forgotten her fears in the joy of catching up. That night in Paris had seemed like an ideal opportunity to renew their friendship, to discover who they had both become since leaving the orphanage and growing up. So after the charity ball had ended she had gone with him for a leisurely late dinner, and then back to her hotel.

By the time she'd realised her mistake, and that he was longer the inexperienced boy she had known on Calista, it had been too late; the damage had been done.

He was leaner now than he'd been in Paris, dark hair slicked back, his black jeans casual yet perfectly tailored, his white shirt immaculate. He took four or five confident strides away from the helicopter and stopped there, just clear of the blades. As if sensing her gaze on his face, he raised his head, looking towards the orphanage as he began to unbutton his jacket.

'Rafael…' she whispered.

Through whirling dust their eyes met with a force that knocked the breath from her. In that instant she flashed back to a doctor in the hospital, telling her apologetically that her mother was dead and she was alone. The self-same dread crept through her now…the shiver of abandonment.

Momentarily dazzled, as though she'd looked too long

at the sun, Sabrina staggered back a few steps, dazed and disorientated.

Then she turned and fled.

The helicopter had barely touched down before Rafael was out and striding towards the orphanage, unbuttoning his jacket against the familiar Calistan heat. Throwing one swift glance up at the building he had viewed as a prison during his childhood, he checked abruptly at the sight of a pale oval at an upper window.

Sabrina was already there. A ghost in the condemned building.

Of course it didn't have to be her at the window. But then she moved, and he knew her at once. The turn of that blonde head, the light, natural way she moved her hair, like a field of ripe corn dancing in sunlight, rustling and bending with the wind. Everything inside him clenched at the memory of that fair hair spread out on the pillow, her laughing eyes…

Damn it!

Gritting his teeth, Rafael slipped on a pair of reflective sunglasses and kept walking, his face carefully wiped of emotion. He sucked in a sharp breath that he couldn't seem to exhale, his lungs burning as he struggled against emotions he had long since refused to acknowledge. It was one thing to feel such weakness as a child, physically inadequate in the face of his father's cruelty. But he was a man now.

Why the hell had he made this crazy decision to travel halfway across the world to attend this meeting in person? His PA had been right, calling it dangerous and a colossal waste of his time.

'Let me staff it out for you, sir,' Linda had said crisply, plucking Sabrina's letter away to study it for herself. 'Oh, yes, this has trouble written all over it. Andrew Templeton's daughter? Wasn't she the one at that charity ball in Paris?'

Spotting his frown, his PA had adroitly changed tack, snatching up the phone instead.

'Don't worry, I'll ask Christopoulos to deal with her. He's local to Calista and did a good job over the sale of the orphanage.'

None of his other staff would have dared handle him like that. But Linda was fifty-odd, acid-tongued and married with kids, one of them close to his own age. He was one of the youngest billionaire CEOs in New York City, so he valued her experience and even occasionally her maternal instincts.

'No, I'll speak to her myself.' Rafael had signed the paperwork on his desk, pushing his own internal voice of warning to the back of his mind. 'Get the jet fuelled and tell Johannes to file a flight plan to Athens. Have a company helicopter meet us there to fly me over to Calista.'

'Respectfully, sir—'

'The decision's made.' He'd played with his shirt cuffs, thinking hard. 'I'll need Villa Rosa opened up for me too.'

'You're planning a long stay, then?'

'Maybe.'

Rafael had barely known what he was planning at that

stage. But he had known that this might be his only opportunity to meet Sabrina Templeton again face to face.

There was something he had to tell her—a deeply personal communication that could not be made by email or over the phone—and he had put it off long enough. He had no idea how Sabrina might react, and he owed it to his childhood friend to do it gently and in private.

Despite that, he agreed with Linda's astute analysis. Given his history with Sabrina, it was a scenario fraught with danger. Yet once the idea had taken root in his brain, growing with the wiry tenacity of a weed, he'd been unable to shake it loose.

'Sir, your schedule is pretty full-on this month.' Linda had flicked through his calendar app. 'I'm not sure it's practical.'

'Then clear my schedule,' he'd said curtly, dismissing her concerns. 'I'll need a car too. Sort it for me, would you? And call our stables there… Have them take a selection of my horses over to the villa.' Seeing her amazement, he'd given his PA a cool smile. 'Come on, you were only saying yesterday that I needed a break.'

'I meant a weekend in the Hamptons. Not an indefinite stay on a tiny Greek island. Besides, I've seen photos of that villa of yours, built into the cliff. Talk about remote…' Linda had rolled her eyes. 'Not terribly comfortable either, I should imagine, unless you're a Tibetan monk. Remind me, does it have hot and cold running water yet?'

Rafael had grinned appreciatively at his assistant's flippant zingers. 'Actually, it was a monastery back in the day, and I had the place renovated three years ago. Installed a pool and gym and extended the property. There's even plumbing in the kitchen now. No more jogging to the spring every morning for fresh water.'

He'd laughed at her theatrical shudder.

'Relax, would you? I'll fly out there, talk to...' He'd struggled to say her name without showing the turmoil inside. 'To Miss Templeton. And then fly back after a few weeks of sun, sea and snorkelling.'

It might take him that long to recover from facing Sabrina, he had thought grimly.

'What about the monthly board meeting?'

'I'm sure the board can manage without me for once.'

Rafael had shrugged, treading restlessly to the window to stare out across Manhattan. It was a view he'd grown to love since making New York his home nearly ten years ago: sunlight glinting off skyscrapers, a forest of steel and tinted glass everywhere he looked. Although he got the occasional glimpse of the Hudson River when he was walking through the city. He liked seeing that bright flash; it reminded him that this was an island too, albeit very different from the one where he'd grown up.

'Look, why don't you sit in for me at any major meetings? You know where I stand on most things.'

Linda had looked pleased, but queried, 'And the new deal? You can't deny we've hit a roadblock, sir. We could really do with you at the negotiating table.'

Rafael had gritted his teeth at that reminder. They were in the middle of delicate negotiations with a US company founded by an ultra-conservative family. But recent talks had stalled after one of the major shareholders had complained of Rafael's multiple high-profile flings with beautiful women, calling these short-lived affairs 'decadent and outrageous'.

'Tell them I'm working on a solution.'

With that, he'd shrugged into his jacket and headed for the door, his mind already elsewhere—in the dusty sunlit land of his youth, where he and Sabrina had run wild together, two kids bound by the bonds of friendship.

Now here he was, his feet firmly planted on the dry soil of Calista, back at the orphanage where it had all begun for him... The sickening aftermath of his parents' brutal deaths and his long climb out of the depths of poverty.

Rafael eyed the orphanage with creeping abhorrence. He had hated this place for so long he'd demolished it a thousand times in his imagination, or let roses and briars grow up around it like an enchanted castle in a fairy tale.

Then fate had struck. The director of the orphanage had contacted him out of the blue about some renovations, seeking a charitable donation. Rafael had jumped at the chance to buy the place outright and flatten it instead—to bulldozer its cruel walls into oblivion and give the kids there somewhere new to live. A fresh start for the orphans as well as himself.

Somehow Sabrina had got wind of his scheme and put in an objection. Far too late, of course. It was a done deal. The kids had already been moved and the demolition was scheduled for a few weeks' time.

He'd been intrigued by the half pleading, half threatening note of her letter. Her silence for the past five years had been eloquent: she had not forgiven him for

Paris. Yet she felt strongly enough about the orphanage
to break cover and contact him at last. It had seemed the
ideal opportunity for him to do what he ought to have
done years ago and come clean about what he knew.

Since Sabrina was based in London, and he was in
New York, suggesting a meeting at the orphanage itself had struck him as a reasonable compromise. Neu-
tral territory.

Now he was regretting that decision.

His visceral reaction just now, on glimpsing her face
at the window, told him starkly that he wasn't over her.
That he would never be over her. Not after their aston-
ishing night together in Paris. But he could handle Sabrina Templeton, he told himself. He just needed to keep
business at the forefront of his decision-making process.
Not the tug of deep-down desire he still felt whenever
he thought of her.

The front door was ajar. Rafael stalked into the familiar hallway, finding it empty. He stripped off his
sunglasses, pushing them into his top pocket. Head up,
chest out, every inch of him exuded a confidence it had
taken him years to construct.

'Sabrina?' he called. 'I saw you at the window just
now. I know you're in here.' He paused, turning on his
heel. 'Where are you hiding?'

Silence greeted him.

Possessed by a gnawing frustration, he took the stairs
two at a time. He didn't like spending even a few minutes in this godforsaken building. The sooner it was
knocked down the better. His heart was thumping, his
palms damp. Memories dogged his footsteps every inch

of the way. Older boys calling him names, throwing stones and punches… He had always fought back, despite being outnumbered.

There was no sign of her upstairs either. But he heard a distant clatter—like a broom falling. A grim smile touched his lips and he retraced his steps down the stairs.

There was an alcove under the back stairs where cleaning tools used to be stored. There was a low space beyond it, just big enough for a child to crawl into and hide. In their day a filthy curtain had covered it, but someone had replaced this with a low door which now stood closed.

Rafael hesitated, taking a deep breath. As a child, his father had often locked him in a dark cavity under the floor as a punishment. Now he disliked elevators and avoided tight spaces, despising his own weakness but aware that they made him slightly crazy.

Wrenching open the cupboard door, he bent and peered into darkness. The mops and buckets had gone, but there was a dusty broom leaning at an angle, as though hastily replaced. He could see the tips of two elegant shoes poking out of the shadows and heard a disconcerted gasp as her hiding place was violated.

'Sabrina.' He held out a hand to her, as if trying to coax a wounded animal out of hiding. 'Come out,' he said in Greek, instinctively using his native tongue now that he was back on the island where he'd been born. 'This is no place for you.'

Sabrina had often hidden here as a child, when the taunting had grown too much, pulling the curtain across and listening, knees tucked under her chin, while the staff hunted high and low for her. As her closest friend, Rafael had always known where she would be hiding, and had come along once the coast was clear to persuade her out again.

They'd been the two misfits of the orphanage. Sabrina with her scarred face and brooding silences. Rafael with his hot temper and criminal background.

When the other kids had picked on them, Rafael had always acted instinctively to divert attention from Sabrina, had been guilty of fights and breakages. 'Like father, like son,' some of the wardens had sneered at him. Rafael had ignored that lie; he was nothing like his mean, vicious father. But when one older boy had spoken disrespectfully of his mother, mocking him over how she'd died, he had lost control.

After that particular dust-up, the wardens had put him in solitary for a week.

Sabrina had come to visit him, sneaking extra food through the window.

They'd been inseparable as kids.

There had never been anything between them but friendship, of course.

Until that night in Paris…

'Go away, Rafe.'

Her voice was a mere thread of sound.

He repeated his request more firmly, adding, *'Parakalo…'* his voice cracking on that final word, *Please*.

'No,' she whispered.

Her rejection hurt, exactly as it had done the day she'd left him behind, smiling up at Andrew Templeton, her new father, as he steered her out of the orphanage and into the sunlight. Rafael had been happy for her all the same, knowing she was better off with a rich family, and had written her dozens of letters, hoping for news of her life in England.

No reply had ever come.

What a fool he'd made of himself over her. And for what? Sabrina had soon forgotten him, whisked away to a life of wealth and privilege.

'Don't be such a little coward,' he said roughly, pushing the hurt aside. 'You asked me to meet you and here I am.' He lurched forward and, despite his claustrophobia, stretched his whole arm into the space, his hand rigid and wide-fingered, hunting about for her. 'So you might as well stop hiding in the dark, obsessing over how hard your life has been. Because I can tell you now: mine has been harder.'

'Oh!'

There was outrage in that tiny explosion of sound, and then Sabrina came squeezing out of her hiding place on all fours, a flushed and indignant goddess with dishevelled blonde hair.

She clambered to her feet, knocking away his hand with violent disdain. They faced each other in the echoing hallway. Her breasts were heaving in a white dress that was wholly unsuitable for rustic Calista, its expensive clinging silk smudged with dust. Despite Paris, it was still a shock to see the cool oval of her face smooth and unmarked, no longer the scarred face he'd known and loved as a child. The plastic surgeons had done their work well.

'How dare you?' she ranted, standing almost eye to

eye with him in stylish stilettos that emphasised her slender ankles and long legs.

Yes, Sabrina had grown up, all right.

'You of all people should know…'

Then her voice died away as their eyes met.

CHAPTER TWO

SHE HAD FORGOTTEN how his presence tugged at her. Though it was mostly a physical allure now they had grown up. God, yes, it *was* physical. That sharp tilt to his cheekbones, his broad chest and shoulders, the long, athletic legs and the arrogant way he held himself...

But the attraction she felt for him dug deeper than mere physical desire. Once it had been friendship—two lost children finding solace in each other's undemanding company. But in Paris their friendship had shifted abruptly to something more profound. The hurt in her had resurfaced and reached out to his own pain, hearing it answer her cry. And making love that night...

It had been a revelation. Like finding the lost half to a broken bowl and fitting the two pieces together so perfectly you knew it would hold milk again and never spill.

'Hello, Sabrina,' he was saying, still in the Greek island dialect they had both spoken as children. 'It's good to see you again.'

Then Rafael paused, long dark lashes sweeping down to hide the expression in his eyes.

'Know what, exactly?' he asked.

'I beg your pardon?' she said huskily, thrown off balance, trying not to let her hunger show in her face.

'You said, *"You of all people should know..."* but then you didn't finish.'

His dark eyes were deep, velvety wells of blackness that urged her to fall in and willingly drown herself.

'What is it I'm supposed to know? Or is this another of your elaborate guessing games?'

She caught a hint of bitterness on the end of that question and stiffened, instantly on her guard. In Paris, she had gone to bed with the Rafe she'd known and loved for years, ignoring the alarm bells that came with his pleasure-seeking reputation, and woken up with a stranger—a man who'd spoken to her in a voice full of light contempt and walked out of her life, leaving her hollowed out like a breakfast egg, all brittle shell and emptiness.

'I don't want to be reminded of the past, Sabrina,' he'd told her on the phone, heading to the airport for his flight back to New York. 'You were a part of the old Rafael, and all I want in my life is what still lies ahead. The future.'

Left alone, she'd flown back to the rainy streets of London in more agony than she could remember feeling since the accident that had claimed her mother's life. But she had emerged from that refining fire as a new Sabrina, colder and harder, the last vestiges of her innocence ripped away by one wild night of passion.

Rafael was waiting for an answer, his eyes locked on hers.

'That I'm not a coward,' she told him, switching

abruptly to English and tilting up her chin when his lips compressed into a thin line. 'That's what you should know. Also, I wasn't obsessing over how hard my life has been. I got lucky here. I was rescued.'

'Unlike me?' he suggested, also in English, with the faint hint of an American accent behind his words.

Again their gazes clashed.

'No, you're a self-made man,' Sabrina admitted. 'And that's something to be proud of. You made it on your own and worked hard to be successful.'

'Damn right I did,' he said, almost between his teeth.

'I haven't had everything handed to me on a plate, if that's what you think. My father...' She hesitated, seeing an odd expression in his face and realising too late what she had said. 'My *adoptive* father,' she corrected herself carefully, 'made sure I wanted for nothing. But he didn't make it easy for me either. I've had to fight for what I wanted. Prove I'm worthy of—'

'His love?' he supplied when she paused.

'Of course not,' she snapped, instantly protective of the kindly, generous man who had adopted her. 'Not everything in this world has to be dog-eat-dog. Of course Andrew Templeton loves me—as I love him. We're father and daughter, even if that's a legal position, not one based on genetics. I was going to say worthy of his *support*.'

It was true that her adoptive father was capable of withholding love at times—usually when he disapproved of her choices—and even of stomping on her feelings if she dared exhibit any. But he meant it for the best.

'The world of business is tough,' her father often said,

'especially for women. You've got to be tough in return, Sabrina. Show no emotion…even when it's going badly.'

Andrew Templeton had given her money, opportunity, a roof over her head. But she'd still needed to work hard to earn his approval. Luckily, that had never been a problem for her. She enjoyed the challenge. Hard work kept her demons at bay.

'So he'll agree to bankroll your projects,' Rafael said flatly.

Sabrina gritted her teeth against a rising tide of fury. 'I enjoy bringing new opportunities to Andrew's attention, yes. But they're all profit-makers. It's a quid pro quo.'

'Spare me,' Rafael said, and turned on his heel, stalking away.

'Hey, where are you going?' Impatient, she strode after him, elegant heels clicking loudly on the stone flags. 'I haven't finished.'

He didn't stop or look back, and Sabrina found her gaze drawn to his fast-moving body.

Stop ogling him, she told herself crossly.

But it was impossible when the black denim of his well-cut jeans hugged his taut behind and outlined his muscular thighs as he walked—a sight which soon had her thinking of one thing only… How his lean body had felt, sliding over hers that night in Paris, skin against skin, her desperate fingers pinioning his flesh against her.

'Why did you come here today, Rafe, if you're not even prepared to talk to me?' She threw the words at his back.

The question brought him to a halt at last. He turned, dark eyes glittering in the gloom.

They had reached the hallway. The front door stood open, heat and fragrance drifting in from the overgrown sunlit gardens outside. The sun was rising higher in the sky, and already she could feel sweat breaking out on her back, the white silk clinging stickily to her skin.

She ought not to have picked such a revealing dress today. But she'd wanted to make a bold statement at this meeting…just in case he turned up. She'd wanted Rafael to know she was his equal now—a hard-nosed CEO, too worldly-wise to roll over at his command.

Then she'd run and hidden like a scared child.

He must have read her mind, for his gaze narrowed before dropping over her bare shoulders in the strapless white dress and then, disconcertingly, moving even lower.

'Why did you hide from me under the stairs?' he tossed back at her in turn. 'Like a wild rabbit fleeing in terror for some hole in the ground.'

Angry colour bloomed in her cheeks. 'As you said, Rafael, it was a game. Hide-and-Seek, like in the old days.' Her smile was false but she thought he might buy it. 'I wanted to see if you remembered my favourite hiding place.'

'How could I forget?' he replied slowly, still looking her up and down.

There was a restless heat in his eyes that Sabrina recognised from last time. She turned away to avoid that devouring look, heading out instead into the hot, cicada-rich morning.

'It's so peaceful here,' she said hurriedly, to hide her discomfort. 'A beautiful building in picturesque surroundings. I can't believe anyone in their right mind would wish to knock it down. Not when you could so easily turn it into a hotel or a community centre. Maybe even a museum.'

She turned abruptly, startled to find that he'd followed her outside and was standing close, only inches away. But she refused to be intimidated.

His hands were thrust into his pockets, his eyebrows tugged together in a frown, and he was looking back at her stonily. Her heart sank at that closed demeanour. She had negotiated enough business deals to know the signs of someone determined not to budge.

She met the challenge of that obsidian gaze head-on, trying to break through his defences with a cry from the heart. And her heart *was* crying. Both at the demolition of the past and at what they'd become to each other. Once so intimate, now deadly enemies. And she had no idea how they'd got there.

'Why did you come here today?' she repeated. 'In person, I mean. It's a long flight from New York. Why not send a flunky?'

He did not answer at first, then he said slowly, 'I was curious to hear what you had to say, that's all.' His face was shuttered, harder to read than ever. 'So far, it's the same tired argument I've already heard.'

'Because I haven't given you my personal view,' she said earnestly, trying to appeal to the old Rafael—the one she hoped was still in there somewhere, if only she could reach him. 'I want to preserve this building because it represents love. Love and protection. Good people looking after children who have nobody else in the world.'

She saw the flicker of hostility in his eyes and took a deep breath.

'Okay, I can see I've touched a nerve. You didn't get an easy ride here. I remember the bullying you faced. But the wardens took you in and cared for you, didn't they?'

A low blow, perhaps, but she had to get through to him. He'd been a rebellious, wayward child, but with good reason. His father had been an Italian drug dealer who'd shot his Greek wife and then killed himself, all when Rafael was only ten years old. After that Rafael had claimed his life was cursed. But he must have broken the curse—else how could he have become such a successful and powerful man, outwardly a million miles from that troubled boy from a lawless family?

'I didn't come here to reminisce about the old days,' he said bluntly. 'The point is, this place is obsolete. Today's Calistan orphans want to live somewhere more modern.'

He paused, running a finger inside the collar of his white shirt, as though uncomfortable in the rapidly increasing heat of the day. They had both grown accustomed to the luxury of air-con, she thought wryly, feeling much the same discomfort herself and realising she had barely noticed this heat as a child.

'They want Wi-Fi and big bathrooms and a skate park,' he went on.

'So you say. I'd like to hear the kids themselves tell

me that. And if it's true, why not rehouse the kids but leave this old place in peace?' she pushed on, sensing a shift in him. 'I know you struggled to get permission to knock the orphanage down. Why not sell it to me instead? Or consider alternatives to demolition? A sympathetic redevelopment, for instance?'

'Because I hate it,' he said hoarsely, shocking her. And then stopped, his jaw set hard. He looked away, his lashes once more hiding his expression.

Sabrina did not know what to say. He *hated* the orphanage?

'Forgive me,' he continued stiffly, after a moment's silence. His accent was harsh, and yet flowing at the same time, like water running over boulders in a mountain stream, his half-Greek, half-Italian heritage making itself known. 'I accept that you feel differently. But this place is mine now and it's my decision to make. The building has structural issues and it's coming down.'

'Structural issues that could be fixed with a little investment.'

When he didn't respond, Sabrina stared at him in despair, wishing she could break through that tough façade.

'I don't understand. Why do you hate this place so much? I always thought—'

He raised dark brows at her, his expression fierce. 'That I was *happy* here?'

The interruption was almost a slap. She took a few seconds to steady herself.

'That *we* were happy here,' she corrected him softly, her gaze searching his face. 'Rafe…'

He took a step closer at the sound of his name, his

eyes locked with hers, and she instantly recoiled, unable to help herself. The thought of him touching her was too much to bear.

Rafael checked at her recoil, his mouth thinning into a smile so bleak it made her shiver.

'So that's why you ran to hide when you saw me arrive.' There was zero emotion in his tone. 'I repulse you. Yet you were so responsive that night in Paris…as though you'd never been touched before.'

He reached out, one fingertip brushing her cheek. She felt a rush of heat there and knew she was blushing.

'Ah…' He let out his breath in a long sigh. 'We were perfect for each other at sixteen,' he continued softly, 'long before we knew what to do with those feelings. Now we know, but it's too late.'

His gaze tangled with hers. She could smell honeysuckle on the warm air, drifting in from the gardens, its fragrance heavy and sweet, drugging her senses.

His dark eyes grew sensual under heavy lids, moving over her again. 'Or maybe not.'

Why had she ever thought his eyes were like black stone? They were dark, shifting pools, reflecting her startled expression.

She swallowed and took a shaky breath, struggling to break free of his spell. 'I don't know what you're talking about.'

'Liar,' he said, and gave a short laugh when she spun away.

'I want to save Calista Orphanage,' she said. 'Is that such a terrible thing? You may hate this place, but I love it with all my heart, and I still believe it's a beautiful place for children to grow up.' She looked back at him in hopeless yearning. 'Sell it to me, Rafe. I couldn't bear to see it torn down. It reminds me of happier days.'

He came close and she could smell his maleness now, in the alluring citrus scent of his aftershave, and she caught the faint shadow of stubble on his strong jaw.

'"Happier days"?' he echoed grimly. 'About that...' Rafael drew breath, as though to say something further and then stopped, his brows tugging together.

She waited, watching in puzzlement. What was on his mind?

'Let me get this straight. You love the orphanage *with all your heart*?' he quoted, his speculative gaze on her face. 'You'd do anything to get it?'

'Yes,' she agreed, aware of how weak that admission made her in his eyes.

But this was Rafael. Despite Paris, the past still bound them together. She could trust him.

'In other words, there's something you want here and only *I* can give it to you,' he mused, and now the glittering black stone was back in his eyes, blocking her every attempt to read his thoughts. 'Maybe we could trade.'

There—it was done.

The suggestion had been thrown out there so lightly, so carelessly, as though it weighed nothing. And yet the inherent danger had his whole body tingling with shock, his breath trapped in his throat.

His original intention had been to reveal what he knew about her past and then get back into the helicopter and fly across the island to his villa, for a few weeks of rest and relaxation by the pool. He certainly had no wish to waste any more time in this hateful place, mesmerised by mussed-up blonde hair as it trailed over the bare shoulder of this woman in a knock-out white dress held up by nothing more than the impressive anchor point of her breasts.

Yet, however hard his emotions snapped at him to complete this unpleasant task and get the hell out of there, his cold, logical business brain was busy formulating a more strategic plan.

'Excuse me?'

It seemed Sabrina hadn't got his barely veiled proposition. Or was pretending she hadn't understood.

'You want a stay of execution for the orphanage.' He smiled. 'And I'd like a chance to make up for what happened in Paris. I shouldn't have cut things short. I see that now. It's become…unfinished business.'

Her eyes flashed and she took a quick step backwards. No, she hadn't forgotten Paris either. He'd hurt her pride. No woman liked to be dumped. But he'd been in danger—serious, gut-wrenching danger—of losing his head over her. Something he'd sworn never to do with any woman. A terrifying thought had crossed his mind on waking up beside Sabrina, and he'd known he had to get out of there straight away.

Now, though, he could see a way to solve two problems with one solution.

An alarm bell was ringing insistently at the back of his head but he ignored it. Nobody was on fire. Not yet, at any rate.

His groin tightened at the thought.

'What do you say, Sabrina?' he asked huskily. 'How about a quid pro quo?'

He was deliberately echoing what she'd said earlier about her relationship with Templeton—the billionaire businessman with a finger in so many pies nobody knew exactly what his empire stood for, except that it was huge, a global web of companies with one man at the heart of it, constantly spinning straw into gold.

A quid pro quo. One thing in exchange for something else. Nobody being cheated…everybody winning.

'Let me get this straight.' The blue of her eyes had darkened. 'You want me to…?' She licked her lips as he took a step closer, and his gaze narrowed on the nervous movement. 'What? Spend the night with you again? Like we did in Paris?'

'Tempting,' he drawled, his heart beating erratically at the memory. 'That *was* quite a night.'

Part of him wanted to drag her into his arms and kiss her, see if lightning would strike twice. But once the stopper was drawn out of that particular genie's bottle he wasn't sure he'd be able to contain the explosion. No, it was better to keep his distance physically.

Besides, he still had something to tell her—the kind of bombshell you couldn't simply drop on a good friend and walk away. This way he could bide his time. Pick the moment carefully.

'But a one-night stand is always so unsatisfactory, don't you think?' he added, and saw her flinch.

She said nothing in response, her gaze dropping away. Rafael tried to read her expression and failed.

Into the burning silence, he said persuasively, 'Look,

enough messing around. How about I put a serious deal on the table? Something that will meet your needs as well as my own?'

They were standing very close, almost touching. The fragrant heat off her body was driving his senses crazy… His pulse was racing, his mouth dry with longing.

'What kind of deal?' she asked suspiciously.

Did he dare make the offer he was so impulsively contemplating? It was off-the-chart outrageous. But hell, why not throw it out there and see what the reaction was? It would be the perfect solution to his current difficulties.

'Marry me.'

'What…? What did you say?'

She seemed stunned by his husky command—as well she might be. It was a fantastical proposal, of course it was. And yet he meant it.

Her lips parted, as though she was sensing the seriousness of his intent, and her eyes widened, a confused, storm-tossed blue. 'You must be mad.'

'You want the orphanage. I'll sell it to you in exchange for…' He drew an unsteady breath, not quite believing he was actually going to say it. 'My wedding ring on your finger.'

Her eyes widened even more and grew turbulent. 'Don't mock me, Rafe.'

'It's no joke.'

He needed to move this conversation to negotiation level, he realised, seeing her accusing expression, and he effortlessly shifted gear.

'I'm embroiled in a business deal with a deeply conservative US company,' he explained, his tone matter-of-fact, 'and they've made their objections to me plain. The playboy reputation…my refusal to settle down… Their doing business with me is making their stakeholders nervous.' He paused. 'My advisors tell me marriage would silence their concerns.'

There was a pulse jerking in her throat. 'So get married. Any woman would do. You don't need me.'

'On the contrary—you're the perfect choice. Intelligent, presentable, quick-thinking. A wife who understands the high-pressure world I live in.'

'Sounds like you ought to marry your secretary,' she snapped.

'My PA is already happily married.'

His gaze flickered over her, punctuated by another hot stab of desire that he ruthlessly suppressed. Once they were married he would get used to looking at her and that problem would go away on its own.

'Besides,' he added pointedly, 'I need a woman who can grace my arm on red carpet occasions, and while Linda is a wonderful wife and mother, she's not one for high heels and ballgowns. In fact, there's a public event coming up soon that would be perfect for us to attend together,' he mused. 'It would certainly get the paparazzi talking.'

'Stop it, Rafe. I'm not going to marry you and that's final.'

Swiftly, he foregrounded her needs. 'Look, do this and you can keep your precious orphanage.' He dangled that prize in front of her and saw how tempted she was. 'I'll gift you the deeds as soon as the ink's dry on the certificate. You can do whatever you want with the building. Move the kids back in or redevelop it for your own uses.' He waited, impatient now for her agréement. 'Well? Is it a yes or a no?'

'This isn't fair. You're…pushing me.' Chewing on her luscious lower lip, Sabrina ran a hand through her wayward blonde hair. 'Anyway, I don't understand… I thought you hated this place—that you were determined to demolish it.'

Rafael gritted his teeth, considering that. Yes, he would have rejoiced to see the orphanage torn down, brick by brick. Its existence reminded him of all those taunts about his weakness as a boy, his inability to look after his mother and stand up to his bullying father.

But he'd been through therapy to deal with those horrors—not entirely successfully—and he was also a businessman. He could see the worth in rejecting one vision for the sake of a better one.

He disliked being quizzed about his background when the majority of his peers were the products of wealth and privilege—not like him, an orphan who'd dragged himself out of poverty through sheer hard work and determination. This marriage of business equals—to a Templeton, of all people—would seal his position in the global community and allow him to move forward with those deals that had been put out of his reach by more traditionally-minded shareholders.

Besides, the orphanage wasn't the only thing in his past that needed to be dismantled. His attraction to Sabrina was another dangerous hangover from that earlier phase of his life. However, familiarity bred contempt, as the saying went. Once Sabrina was his wife, constantly by his side, she would cease to hold the same allure for him, he was sure.

'I can be flexible where necessary, and I'm willing to revise my decision on this.' He raised his brows. 'How about you?'

She looked away without saying a word.

Rafael pressed on, confident in his ability to persuade her. Now that he had voiced his impromptu plan, he could see it was the perfect fix for their problems.

'We'll spend our honeymoon here on Calista. I have a villa on the island—only a few minutes away by helicopter. Villa Rosa. It's quiet, very beautiful, very remote…' He saw her unfocused blue gaze lift to his face and added roughly, before she could protest, 'There's only a few days' wait for a wedding licence on Calista. We can be married as soon as the paperwork's gone through.'

'You're forgetting something,' she said defiantly.

'What's that?'

'I haven't said yes.'

He curbed his frustration, seeking instead to address her concerns. 'What more do you need? My reassurance that this is strictly a business arrangement? That I only need you to attend a few public events as my wife… enough to convince the doubters?'

They were standing so close her sweet, female fragrance tugged at his senses, tangling itself around his heartstrings and jerking hard, making his breath suddenly constricted.

'I can do that,' he said, more slowly. 'In fact, let's make this a paper marriage. I'll have a contract drawn up and we'll both sign.'

'Paper marriage? What does that mean?'

'No sex,' he said briefly, and saw shock in her widening eyes. That had been too blunt for her tastes. 'All you need do is accept my terms,' he added, deflecting her moment of uncertainty, 'and the orphanage is yours, Sabrina.'

His hands had clenched into fists while they were talking. Aware of that tell-tale sign, Rafael consciously relaxed his shoulders, forced his too-tight muscles to loosen, and allowed his facial expression to shift into polite neutrality. Any obvious nerves on his part would only give her the upper hand in this discussion.

Sabrina drew a ragged breath. 'I can't,' she said huskily, and turned away.

Something akin to desperation flashed through him. He had come here to perform a grim task, then managed to talk himself out of it and offer her marriage instead, and now she was refusing him.

'In that case,' he ground out, his jaw clenched against a need so laser-hot it was burning away at his soul: the compulsion to conclude whatever this was between them and move on as fast as possible, 'you leave me no choice.'

The words were out before he could take them back.

She spun, staring at him, something in his tone clearly alerting her to the seriousness of this moment. 'What—? What do you mean?'

'I have something to tell you. Something…hard.'

Her chin rose. 'So tell me.'

Rafael knew that stubborn look. His heart went out to her, for he also knew how this information would crush her. But what choice did he have? This secret couldn't be concealed for ever. They had been soulmates once. Better him tell her than a stranger.

'Templeton is your father,' he burst out.

Her smile was crooked. 'Of course he is. He legally adopted me. You were there the day he collected me from the orphanage. So what?'

'No, you don't get it.' His voice dropped, became husky with emotion. 'He really is your father, Sabrina. Your *biological* father.'

CHAPTER THREE

SABRINA'S INSIDES CHURNED with anxiety as she studied his lean, dark face. Rafael seemed serious, and yet… How could he be?

'What on earth are you talking about?' she demanded.

'Wait here a minute, would you?'

He strode off towards the helicopter, leaving her stunned and uncertain on the orphanage steps.

'I'm sick of these games—' she began angrily.

But he called over his shoulder. 'Sabrina, trust me. I'll be right back.'

Irritated, she considered stalking to her car and simply leaving. But something about his ridiculous assertion nagged at her subconscious, and she made the decision to wait, even though she was sure that he was just messing with her head again.

There was a stone bench in the shade of the orphanage walls. She sat there, gazing up at the intense blue sky she remembered from her youth, trying to collect her shattered nerves. Andrew Templeton her biological father? It was simply impossible. Rafael couldn't be serious. Could he?

Two minutes later he was back, his jacket gone, top button loosened, and a fawn-coloured dossier in his hands.

'Here,' Rafael said, handing her the dossier, 'this is for you.' He ran a restless hand through his short dark hair. 'There's no easy way to say this, but… Templeton has been lying to you. And this is the proof.'

'Lying to me about what?'

He nodded to the dossier in her hand. 'Everything's in there.'

Sabrina stared up at him, fury and disbelief tugging her brows together. 'Rafael, if this is your way of discrediting the man who's been responsible for shaping my life since—'

'Read the dossier,' he insisted, cutting her off. 'Look at the printouts. The emails and letters he exchanged with the orphanage director. I found them here after I acquired the building. I've collected newspaper cuttings too— plus the results of a private investigation I ordered once I'd realised what I was looking at. It's all there. Witness statements, flight records, charitable donations…' His voice deepened. 'Details of Templeton's visits to Calista before you were even born,' he added grimly, 'and again in the years prior to your adoption.'

She still didn't believe a word of it. But she was curious to see what evidence he could possibly have gathered to prove this ludicrous assertion.

Reluctantly, she began to flick through the dossier. Her body stiffened and she turned back a few sheets, rereading the documents more carefully.

'Oh, my God…' she whispered. Her eyes flew to his

face, horrified, and then she returned to the dossier. 'This can't be true.'

'I wanted to tell you earlier,' he said huskily. 'But I knew it had to be done discreetly, in person, and away from your father. Templeton would have stopped me speaking to you if he'd got wind of my discovery. And I meant that offer of marriage, by the way. If you'd said yes, I would have picked my moment to tell you about your father. As it is… I'm sorry.'

Rolling up his sleeves, he left her to read the dossier in peace, seating himself a short distance away on the orphanage steps.

'Let me know when you're done.'

Sabrina's hands shook as she read, her hope that it might be a lie soon fading. The billionaire who had rescued her from poverty and transported her so miraculously to a life of luxury beyond her wildest imaginings was not the hero she had always thought him to be. In fact, he was a liar and a cheat—and her biological father.

It was a simple tale.

Andrew Templeton had come to Calista as a wealthy man on a business tour of the Greek islands. Hiring a private villa, he'd entertained his business associates with wild parties that had turned into full-blown orgies, according to the investigator's report. A year later he'd returned to the island and spent time with an English-woman, Cherie, an ex-pat who'd lived on the island and had recently given birth to a daughter. Soon afterwards she'd been seen driving a new car and wearing expensive clothes, even though she was out of work.

A decade later, following the terrible car crash that

had killed Cherie and left her daughter scarred for life, the girl had been taken in by the orphanage on Calista. A large anonymous donation had been made to the orphanage at around the same time—a donation repeated annually for as long as the girl remained there. This money trail led back to Templeton's first company, AT Holdings.

Emails exchanged between the orphanage and an unnamed executive at AT Holdings revealed the secret instruction that the girl was to be kept at the orphanage and never adopted, with any prospective parents warned off, while further substantial payments to the director and some of the wardens had been made privately, no doubt to ensure their silence and co-operation.

In the same year that his wife Barbara had died of cancer Templeton had returned to Calista, visiting the orphanage in person. Declaring himself enchanted by the sixteen-year-old Sabrina, he had whisked her back to England to become his 'adopted' daughter in the eyes of the world.

With a crash, the heavy dossier fell from Sabrina's hands, papers scattering about her feet. She sat with her head bowed, a curtain of golden hair hiding her face.

A pair of shining black shoes appeared in her line of vision. Then Rafael was kneeling beside her, his hand on hers.

'You okay?' he whispered.

'Of course I'm not. Andrew Templeton is my real father.' Her voice faltered as she said those words out loud for the first time and felt their cruel sting. 'But why lie about it? Why the elaborate pretence? The whole adoption charade? Why didn't he just tell the truth?'

'Templeton was already married when he met your mother,' Rafael pointed out. 'Your brother Tom would have been five at the time, your sister Pippa only two. From my investigations, it seems to have been a whirlwind affair with your mother. But although he supported her financially after your birth, there was never any suggestion that he would acknowledge you publicly as his daughter, despite his insisting on a paternity test… Which proved, of course, that he was your father.'

He paused, and she flung back her curtain of hair, staring into his face at last.

'Even after his wife died and Templeton came to find you, he must have decided to keep your true identity secret to avoid a scandal,' he added. 'And to spare his other children pain and embarrassment.'

'And what about *my* pain? *My* embarrassment?' Sabrina dragged her hand away from his. 'I was the one left to rot in an orphanage for years while my billionaire father ignored my existence.'

'I know.'

Horrible realisations were rushing through her mind one after the other, and she gasped. 'Everyone thought he was so kind…adopting an ugly little orphan girl that nobody else wanted, fixing my scars, helping me into the business world. Instead, he was just *gaslighting* me.' Her hands clenched into fists. 'He did it all out of guilt.'

'I expect Templeton thought you'd hate him if you ever found out the truth.'

She jumped to her feet, unable to sit still a moment

longer, treading carelessly through the scattered papers. How could Andrew Templeton have done this to her? To his own daughter…his flesh and blood. Every bit as much his child as Tom or Pippa.

Fury flooded her. 'What I can't forgive is how he instructed the orphanage director to put off any prospective parents and lie to me about it. To say nobody wanted to adopt me because…because of my…scars.'

A scalding tear rolled down one cheek. Gulping back a sob, she bent to pick up one of the sheets, holding it out to him.

'Did you read this?'

'I've read the whole dossier…cover to cover.'

'A local doctor suggested cosmetic surgery after a check-up on my facial scarring. And Templeton said no. He said it was b-b-better to leave me as I was…so nobody would look twice at me.'

She was sobbing now.

'Come here.'

Rafael took her in his arms and she did not resist, comforted by the reassuring embrace of an old friend. The boy he'd used to be was showing at last through the ruthless mask of the billionaire.

'I'm sorry,' he said softly, close to her ear.

'For what?'

'For causing you such pain.'

'No, I…I'm glad you told me.'

Sabrina swallowed what felt like a throatful of broken glass and took a deliberate step back. Without a word, he released her. Wiping her damp face with the back of her hand, she turned away and sucked in several deep breaths, struggling to get herself back under control.

'What I don't understand is why you didn't take this dossier to Templeton. He would have paid you a fortune to suppress it.' She glanced round at him. 'Maybe even smoothed your way with those narrow-minded conservatives of yours.'

His mouth compressed into a thin line. 'You seriously think I'd have used your pain to blackmail my way into the big boys' club?'

She shook her head. 'No, of course not. I'm sorry. That was unfair of me.' She ran a hand through her hair, turning away. 'But things are starting to make sense at last. The way the wardens treated me so kindly. Why the director always favoured me above the other kids.' Her voice wobbled. 'Because my father was paying them a fortune to keep me prisoner here.'

'Say the word. I'll hunt Templeton down and punish him for this.'

She stopped pacing and turned to look at him wonderingly. 'You'd really do that for me? Go to my father and—?'

'Make him suffer?' Rafael finished for her in a low voice, his gaze on her face. 'You know I would. We're still friends, aren't we? What hurts you, hurts me.'

'Yes… That civilised air doesn't go much deeper than your designer wardrobe, does it?'

As a kid, whenever she'd been bullied, he would chase after her tormenters and then spend hours in solitary for fighting them. All on her account.

'Scratch the expensive surface and it's the old Rafe under there.'

He said nothing, but his face darkened and he thrust both fists into the pockets of his black jeans, straining the material.

'But no,' she continued slowly, 'I can think of a better way to make my father suffer.'

He waited, brows raised.

'Let's do it,' Sabrina said daringly, not quite able to believe the way her thoughts were going.

She took a few steps towards him, swaying on her high heels, her hands twisting together.

'Let's get married. If there's one thing Andrew Templeton can't stand, it's another man taking away his possessions.' She swallowed. 'And I'm one of his possessions, aren't I?'

She met his startled gaze, hoping he hadn't changed his mind after her stark refusal earlier. Rafael might have behaved like a prize bastard in Paris. And he only wanted a wife so he could clean up his image for business purposes—not because he intended to stop playing the field. But she knew this man inside-out, faults and all, and he had brought her this information rather than use it as leverage against Templeton, which would have been more to his advantage.

Right now, she needed someone in her life she could completely trust.

Better the devil you know. Wasn't that the saying?

'If your marriage deal is still on the table, that is?' she added.

* * *

The helicopter rose slowly above the orphanage, rotor blades whirring, and soon they were leaving the old familiar buildings behind, along with her hire car.

Sabrina gripped the seat as they climbed into the sky, her stomach lurching. She often flew in helicopters now, but was never truly comfortable in them. In the window glass she caught her own scar-free reflection and was momentarily shocked, sucking in a startled breath.

Coming back to the orphanage and seeing Rafael again had messed with her head. For a second she'd half expected to see the old Sabrina looking back at her, her face scarred and, to her mind, unsightly. The terrified child who had crawled out of the raging inferno of her mother's wrecked car after it had plunged off the cliff road.

'Freak!' the kids at the orphanage had used to shout, seeing her burns, and it had taken all her persuasion to prevent Rafael from punching them for it.

He had seemed surprised just now, when she'd changed her mind and agreed to his absurd marriage proposal.

'Just to be clear…you're agreeing to be my wife?' he'd asked, eyes narrowed.

'If that's what it takes to get the orphanage.' She had hesitated. 'But only if we can include a time limit clause.'

He had stared at her. 'Meaning?'

'I'll marry you for one year. Then I want a no-contest divorce.' She had glared when he'd begun to protest. 'I'm not chaining myself to you for ever, Rafe. One year will be perfectly sufficient to get under my father's skin and sort out your issues with those conservative businessmen.'

She had stuck out her hand.

'Deal?'

It had not been an easy offer to make. Her heart had been hammering violently and she'd found it hard to breathe. Accepting his proposal was insanely dangerous, both for her heart and her psyche. But she wanted that damn orphanage, and if marrying Rafael would also drive her duplicitous father crazy it made the deal suddenly more attractive.

Besides, it was only for one year.

It went against the grain to make a marriage commitment with a divorce date already lined up. She had always intended to marry for love, positive that she would know and recognise that 'for ever' feeling when she found it. Yet nobody in her life had even come close to the overwhelming, sheet-clawing passion she'd felt with Rafael in Paris.

Except his desire had been for the new and improved Sabrina, the one with perfect skin, not the person she still was deep inside… Which made it all wrong—an off note in a beautiful song, jarring her psyche whenever she thought of it.

Rafael had hesitated a fraction of a second before shaking her hand with a crisply delivered, 'Very well. One year and then we'll divorce. Now, let's get out of this place. It's going to be a busy few days.'

Rafael had gone off with his mobile to hustle through the paperwork and organise the return of her hire car, while she'd called the hotel to settle her bill and arrange the collection of her belongings. She was too accustomed to her father's own high-handed behaviour to question the lightning speed with which this marriage plan was being executed.

But as he'd escorted her to where the helicopter waited in the hot sun his hand had brushed her back and she'd stiffened, turning to face him, sharp as a rattlesnake.

'I've agreed to be your wife,' she'd reminded him coldly, 'not your lover. A paper marriage, you said. No hands, Rafe. Or the deal's off.'

A line of dark red along his bronzed cheeks, Rafael had grimaced. 'Forgive me. It won't happen again.' He'd opened the helicopter door for her. 'You have my word.'

Her response had been partly electric shock—a shiver up the spine that had set her nerve-ends tingling—and partly a test to see how serious he was about this marriage being strictly platonic.

Now, she felt doubly reassured that Rafael could be trusted to keep his side of the bargain. But it was still puzzling. Seated beside him in the helicopter, Sabrina risked a sideways glance at his profile and wondered again at his motives.

Since making his first million in shipping, Rafael Romano had grown into a notorious playboy, his name linked with a series of beautiful models, actresses, even elite sportswomen.

Most recently, he'd been seen out with a professional snowboarder, and Sabrina had winced, scrolling through a few jokey memes about the couple on social media. She'd switched off her phone after reading about their affair and lain down with a headache, wishing she didn't care so much and that he meant nothing to her.

She, on the other hand, had made the decision after Paris not to bother with men again. It simply wasn't worth the anguish when things went sour. Not that she'd had much experience of men before that night with Rafael. Her father had taken pains to shield her from the world after she'd left the orphanage, even hiring a bodyguard to follow her everywhere as a college student. And he'd never allowed her to write to her old friends back on Calista.

'You need to think of your future,' Andrew Templeton had told her early on, after settling her in his luxurious English mansion. Expressionless, he had read and then torn up the letter she'd written to Rafael. 'Those orphan kids are in your past. Besides, they won't want to know you now. Unless they want money out of you.'

'That's not true,' she'd insisted, horrified by such cynicism.

Yet when she'd finally managed to post a few letters secretly to Rafael, care of the orphanage, he had never written back. After several years of silence she had given up and tried to put him out of her mind.

Once she'd left business school, her father had put any prospective boyfriends through such a rigorous grilling that none had ever asked her out on a second date. Even now, whenever she started seeing anyone, Andrew Templeton would find an excuse to interfere.

'It's for your own good, darling,' he would say.

It was true that he had managed to steer her away from fortune-hunters and undercover journalists. Yet his attitude towards her dating anyone had always been conservative and patriarchal in the extreme, and it was only now, knowing what she did about her true parentage, that she saw through his veneer of 'caring' to the coercive, controlling behaviour that lay beneath.

Meeting Rafael again in Paris had been a watershed moment for her. Far from her father's oppressive influence, she'd been bowled over by Rafael's charm and good looks, and sweetly nostalgic for the lost days of her childhood in Calista. She'd tumbled eagerly into bed with him—only to wither and die inside when he'd walked out of her life the next morning without a backward look.

Her faithful companion in dark times as a girl had rejected her after one night together. It had been hard to recover from that blow.

Thanks to her father's over-protectiveness and her own shy hesitancy she had been a virgin with Rafael. It had been the most magical moment, giving herself to him and discovering a hitherto unsuspected world of pleasure in his arms. She had woken the next day shy and smiling, sure they would spend the rest of their lives together...

'What are you thinking?' Rafael asked now, raising his voice over the roar of the rotor blades, his dark gaze on her face. 'Last-minute regrets?'

Sabrina shook her head. 'Not if this marriage teaches my father a lesson. He can't control me any more, and it's about time I made that clear.'

His jaw tightened but he turned his head, looking away across the beautiful green-gold landscape of

Calista. She wondered what was going on inside that heavily defended mind of his. Apart from the emotion-free *kiss, conquer, move on* attitude she'd read about rather too often in the gossip columns.

At least that wild night in Paris had not resulted in a pregnancy. Her periods had always been erratic, and her doctor had suggested taking the pill to regulate them. So when they'd made love that night she'd known herself to be safe. Rafael had not held back after she'd admitted that she was on the pill, perhaps assuming she must have been with other men before him. He had certainly given no sign that he'd known she was a virgin.

They were flying along the barely inhabited western coastline of the island, passing sun-bleached rocks washed by the blue sparkle of the Aegean, only a few isolated dwellings to be seen.

There was a large, whitewashed villa in the distance, built in a quasi-Eastern style, with elaborate archways and a section of domed roof, perched on a crag high above the sea. On the sea-facing side a pool had been built into the cliffs, its blue oblong dazzling against a white surround, a few loungers set around it at intervals under striped umbrellas. The whole place looked beautiful and luxurious…and eerily remote.

'Villa Rosa?' she asked, pointing.

Rafael nodded, following her gaze. 'I phoned ahead and asked the housekeeper to prepare a guest room for you. Your bags should arrive later this afternoon, so you can change into something more comfortable.'

After a quick glance at her revealing white dress—a

look that made her shiver—he settled a pair of reflective sunglasses over his eyes, blocking his expression.

'I'm told the official paperwork should be processed within a few days,' he said. 'Then we can marry. Thankfully, the rules are more relaxed here than on the mainland.'

Only a few days.

Her breath hitched but she said nothing.

'It's important to make a splash with the wedding,' he continued, 'but without risking your father trying to put a stop to it.'

She knew this was no idle concern. If her father got wind of their impending nuptials he would certainly find some way to interfere—legal or not—or at least to postpone the ceremony while he raked up dirt on her proposed bridegroom. She knew Andrew Templeton would not be above using Rafael's unfortunate family history to destroy him in the eyes of the business community if he could possibly manage it.

Part of her longed to confront her father over the way he'd treated both her and her mother. But she knew she would only lose her temper. The emotions churning inside her were still too raw. She was determined to keep her dignity and speak to him calmly, as an adult and an equal, not as the badly hurt child she was inside. But preparing for such a difficult conversation would take some time.

Besides, until the deeds to the orphanage were safely in her hands she dared not risk her father derailing their arrangement with some unexpected manoeuvre.

'What do you suggest?'

'We should marry somewhere even he would find it difficult to access,' Rafael mused. 'I have a large yacht moored at Piraeus that we could use for the ceremony. We'll invite a few trusted members of the media, but only if they agree to keep news of our wedding a secret until we're safely on our honeymoon.'

'And we'll spend the honeymoon on Calista?'

'At Villa Rosa, yes,' he agreed, gazing ahead at the property. 'It's secluded and under twenty-four-hour guard. But we'll tell the paparazzi we're going somewhere else, to throw your father off the scent. The Caribbean, perhaps. I have a small island there that I use occasionally. While everyone's looking in the wrong direction we can relax here without any fear of your father hunting us down.'

Soon they were circling the tiled roofs, and the pilot was instructed by Rafael to make for an area of pasture a safe distance from the house. As they flew over the villa the shadow of the helicopter fell across an inner courtyard with a fountain at its core and a peaceful colonnade, its walkway shaded by leafy green vines.

After landing it was only a short walk through an avenue of dark cypresses to the villa, but Sabrina was fiercely aware of Rafael's presence beside her the whole time. Looking ahead, she focused on the villa instead, admiring its sunny terracotta roof...the whitewashed walls draped in swathes of reddish pink bougainvillea. The path to the front door was lined with pots of tumbling scarlet and yellow flowers, and the air was rich with sweet, heady fragrance.

As they approached the front entrance the door opened

and a stout, smiling woman in a grey and white uniform stepped out to welcome them.

'My housekeeper, Kyria Diakou.'

Politely, Rafael introduced her to Sabrina in Greek, and then listened as the woman, whose first name was Thea, explained the arrangements she had made for their stay and asked if she could bring them anything to eat or drink.

'I propose a light lunch of salad with feta and a bottle of retsina,' he instructed the housekeeper, ushering Sabrina inside a cool hallway with marble floor tiles, its plain white walls decorated with several large, classical style statues and framed gold icons, the saints depicted as bronze-faced and long-lashed as Rafael himself. 'We'll eat outside on the veranda, thank you.'

When Kyria Diakou had hurried away, he led Sabrina into a sitting room dominated by a vast window that overlooked the azure gleam of the Aegean, its blue dotted with speedboats and the white sails of yachts.

'Villa Rosa was a shell when I first bought it,' he told her, walking to the window. 'It's taken years of renovation, and I'm still working on plans for a tennis court. But the privacy and the views…'

'It's beautiful,' she agreed softly.

'I'm glad you like it.' Turning, Rafael came towards her, a slight smile in his eyes, hands outstretched. 'I want you to be happy here.'

As he reached for her Sabrina could not help her instinctive recoil, doing exactly as she'd done before boarding the helicopter. Her heart began to thud wildly.

He stopped and his hands fell back to his sides. 'I

wasn't going to try anything,' he told her grimly. 'I gave you my word.'

'I know. I just…'

It was remembered pain that did it, she realised. The anguish he'd caused her in Paris might be buried deep, but it was still there in her heart.

'Sabrina?' He was still waiting for an explanation, his dark brows tugged together.

'I'm sorry,' she whispered.

Rafael nodded, seeming to consider her apology, then said lightly, 'Forgive me. I've just remembered something urgent I need to do. You'd better eat lunch without me. Just ask Kyria Diakou when she returns,' he added, 'and she'll show you to your room. I'll see you at dinner.'

With that, he strode away.

CHAPTER FOUR

IN TRUTH, HE had nothing urgent to do except brood on the insanity of his impulsive decision to offer her *marriage*, of all things.

In his vast sea-facing bedroom, Rafael found the pristine white covers turned down on his bed and the luggage he'd sent ahead already unpacked, everything hanging ready for him or folded neatly in his walk-in closet. He turned to study the familiar view from his window, his mind still reeling from the enormity of what he'd just done.

Asking her to marry him, out of the blue, and then hitting her with the truth of her parentage when she turned him down.

Small wonder she'd looked so shaken.

Yet she'd said yes.

Before recoiling from him in fear.

Her reaction had hurt. But no doubt he deserved it. Had the way he'd behaved in Paris destroyed the trust between them for ever? Or had he disappointed her in bed that night, so that every time he so much as reached out a hand to her now she would automatically shrink away?

Abruptly, Rafael recalled the violence of his response that night in Paris—his unexpected tears, his head thrown back in agonised pleasure as he climaxed. The emotion had left him floored at the time, unable to comprehend what was happening. Even now he felt strangled, his lungs burning for air, and fought to regain his balance.

Why the hell had he proposed like that?

He had meant simply to tell Sabrina the truth about her father and then walk away from her for ever. Instead, they were going to be married.

He'd always had an issue with impulse control, even after leaving the troubled days of his youth behind. It was something he'd tried to address in therapy over the years. It could be helpful in business, that urge to take crazy risks others might walk away from, but when it came to relationships it was far more damaging. He now had ample proof of that.

Hands in his pockets, he stood at the window for a long while, staring out at the Aegean. It was a view that had always afforded him peace in his high-pressure, trouble-strewn life. He focused on the blue-white haze of the horizon and sought to clear his mind, drawing deep breaths into his lungs and expelling them slowly to a count of ten as he battled to regain some semblance of calm.

But his gaze refused to stay focused on the horizon, dropping instead to the sparkling blue pool set about with sun loungers. He hoped Sabrina would approve of Villa Rosa, though it hardly mattered if she didn't.

Checking his fitness watch, he noted that the calming view was doing nothing for his pulse rate today.

Changing tactics, Rafael stripped off his travel-creased clothes and dragged on fresh black shorts and a T-shirt. Since a meditative state of Zen was apparently impossible to reach with Sabrina under his roof, he would blow off steam in a tough physical workout instead.

Heading down to his newly installed state-of-the-art gym, he was pleased to find everything had been laid out to his exact specifications—a carbon copy of the personal gym in his Manhattan penthouse suite. He set the treadmill timer and pounded away for thirty minutes, as though running from the devil, dripping with sweat and breathing heavily by the end.

He wiped himself down with a plain white towel before hitting the free weights area. Trying to block out the image of Sabrina shrinking from him, fear in her eyes, he hefted barbells to the point of exhaustion and worked out on the floormat with a medicine ball—crucial for maintaining his core strength. Another half-hour later he strode to the shower and doused himself in painfully icy needles of water, grimacing and wishing he could cleanse his mind as easily as his body.

After his workout, he relaxed on his balcony with a stack of magazines on elite cars and motor racing, two of his favourite interests. Yet even they failed to distract him from the throbbing awareness that Sabrina would soon be his wife.

He flicked through the magazines with rigid intent,

studying glossy photographs of racing cars without really seeing them.

It was to be a paper marriage. No sexual contact. Remembering Paris, he reminded himself it would be safer that way. And he could handle it—no problem. He'd never encountered a challenge he couldn't conquer.

Besides, this villa was a former monastery. The perfect environment for embracing his celibate side.

Something about Sabrina triggered his deepest complexes, that was all. Perhaps they'd been so close as kids he still associated her with the early bond he'd felt for his mother. The mother he'd lost so traumatically…

He buzzed down to the staff quarters and asked Nikos Diakou to come up. He was his housekeeper's husband, who oversaw security at the villa, and also worked as chauffeur and gardener. Villa Rosa had an extensive array of cameras and multiple perimeter alarms which Nikos monitored for him. There were also guards discreetly patrolling the exterior of the property while he was in residence.

'I want double the usual number of guards on this visit,' he told Nikos, a smiling, bearded man in early middle age. 'I can't risk any security issues. Not with Miss Templeton here. She is a very special guest.' He hesitated. 'In fact, we're engaged to be married.'

'Congratulations, sir,' Nikos told him, his eyes twinkling, before slipping away to make the arrangements.

When Rafael finally ventured downstairs it was past the dinner hour and Sabrina was waiting for him on the veranda.

Her luggage must have arrived, for she was clad now

in a saffron-yellow wraparound skirt with matching midriff top. There were jewelled sandals on her feet and a silver anklet dangling above one foot, delicate and eye-catching. Leaning on the stone surround that divided the veranda from the pool below, she stood with her face turned towards the sea, her burnished golden hair descending in waves down her back.

The dining table, set under a rustic roof, had been laid for two, silver cutlery glinting, red and white roses artfully arranged in a central display. Champagne was on ice, a thick white napkin wrapped about the bottle.

He stopped in the sliding doorway to admire her rear view. The wraparound skirt fitted snugly, outlining the curves of her tempting behind, while the anklet made him wish to stroke a hand up and down her shapely calf and ankle. A flare of lust lit him from within, but he forced the heat away, aware that she had sensed his presence and was already glancing round to see who was there.

'Oh.' Her hand clutched nervously at the stone balustrade as she met his gaze. 'I didn't hear you open the door.'

'I apologise if I startled you.'

Thee mou! He sounded so formal. Like a stuffed shirt. But her sensual appearance had knocked him off balance again.

She was lightly made-up and looked eminently kissable, especially when her eyes widened, taking in his outfit. He had chosen dark green linen trousers and a pale silk shirt for this evening, worn open-necked. He had decided against sandals, going barefoot instead. The glide of her gaze over his body was like a physical touch, and his arousal stirred again, hard to restrain.

'Wow, that's a very different look for you,' she said. Her cheeks were slightly flushed as she turned fully, her gaze taking in his bare feet. 'I feel distinctly over-dressed.'

'In New York I spend my life in suits and tuxedos. I prefer to dress more casually at Villa Rosa. Feel the ground under my feet. I hope you don't mind the in-formality.'

'No, I'm the same. It will be good to lounge about in flip-flops for a while.'

'I'm sorry to have left you alone all afternoon.' He poured out the champagne and handed her one brim-ming glass, clicking his own against it in a salute. 'To a restful few days. *Yiamas!*'

'*Yiamas...*' she muttered, and downed the entire glass in one long, thirsty swallow. Then she bit her lip, star-ing at him over the champagne flute.

He raised his brows but dutifully refilled her glass and replaced the champagne bottle in the ice bucket.

'Is something wrong?' he asked. The possibility had him frowning. 'Not a problem with your room, I trust?'

'Oh, no, the room is lovely—thank you.' She took only a sip of her champagne this time, her expression suddenly wary. 'It's just…I tried to call my office but there's no mobile signal.'

Rafael couldn't help smiling at her naivety. 'Have you forgotten what life is like on Calista?' He indicated the deep blue Aegean. 'This is one of the least populated of the Greek islands. And Villa Rosa is my refuge from the outside world. No internet, no mobiles, no television or streaming. The housekeeper keeps a satellite phone for her own needs, and so that I can alert her to my visits. But I prefer a clean break. A complete digital detox, I believe it's called.'

Sabrina's eyes hardened, her chin jutting dangerously. 'So, just to be clear, I'm stranded in the middle of nowhere, with no way to call my assistant and let her know where I am or tell her that I'm about to marry a man she's barely even heard me mention.'

'Barely?' he echoed softly.

Not responding to that provocation, she glanced over the balustrade instead, taking in the sheer drop to the sea below. 'I thought by marrying you I'd be escaping my father's obsessive control. But maybe I've jumped out of the frying pan into the fire.' Turning to him, she flicked back her blonde tresses, her look defiant. 'Have I?'

Their eyes met, and something crackled in the air between them—a sudden flash of electricity. He put down his champagne and stalked towards her, torn between anger at her suspicion and humour at this wildly off the mark appraisal.

'You fear I want to control you too?' he demanded.

Sabrina had backed away, coming up against the stone balustrade, her eyes wide, breasts heaving in the tight, shiny yellow top. Heat flared deep inside him and he shifted uncomfortably.

'I didn't say that.'

But her face told him a different story.

'You implied that I'm a tyrant, keeping you shut off from the outside world, when you yourself agreed only a few hours ago to come here of your own accord. Nobody forced you into that helicopter, Sabrina.'

The blue of her eyes matched the restless swell of the Aegean, with darker flecks of defiance and determination within their patina of vulnerability. His gaze dipped to her mouth, a rich bow of shimmering pink, and he struggled against the dangerous impulse to kiss her…to taste that delicious, willing mouth he still remembered.

'But perhaps you need to believe that so you can set me up as the villain of your little fairy tale.'

Sabrina did not move away, staring up at him, wide-eyed.

'Maybe you *want* to be stranded here alone with me,' he continued huskily. 'With nothing to do but relax, swim, sunbathe…and reminisce about the old days.'

His voice, deep and husky, sent shockwaves through her nervous system and made her blood pump faster. Avoiding the complication of any relationship since her last painful encounter with him, Sabrina had begun to consider herself invulnerable to men. Now she realised what a fool she had been. Trying to handle a man like Rafael was like juggling dynamite.

She was fighting for breath, trembling and unsteady before the raw power of his physical attraction. It took all her strength not to turn and flee back to the sanctuary of her bedroom. Since leaving the orphanage, though, Sabrina had learnt not to hide away any more, so she raised her chin and planted her feet instead.

She glared at him. 'Reminisce? I would have thought nostalgic tales about our years at the orphanage were the last thing you wanted to hear.' His eyes narrowed, and she added more coolly, 'But we definitely need to put our heads together and come up with a story to keep my father from suspecting anything. If I don't contact him soon he'll mobilise Interpol to find me. He's very protective, and he likes to know where I am all the time.'

Their eyes clashed, his face was hauntingly close, and for a moment she was struggling to breathe, her voice dying away...

To her relief, though, he turned away and stared out to sea instead, his broad shoulders tense. 'You ride, don't you?' he asked, tangentially.

She blinked, thrown. 'I... Yes, of course.'

'I own a riding stable a few miles from here. A selection of horses is always brought over to the villa for use during my stay. Shall we take a ride out tomorrow morning before it gets too hot?' Rafael swung back to look at her, his gaze once more enigmatic. 'There's a mobile signal further up the coastal road. You could take your phone and contact your father once we're in range, reassure him that you're safe and well. That should keep him off our backs for long enough to put our plan into action.'

Before she could reply, she heard the quiet footsteps of the housekeeper behind her.

'Should I serve dinner now, sir?' the woman asked Rafael in Greek.

He nodded, and she disappeared again.

'It's a good idea to ride out and call my father,' Sabrina agreed.

She was relieved, although her heart was still racing from that unexpected confrontation. It seemed the dangerous moment had passed. For now. Besides, she loved riding and would take great pleasure in exploring the surrounding Calistan countryside on horseback.

'I've brought jeans and boots in my luggage,' she told him. 'But I'll need a riding helmet.'

'I'm sure that can be arranged.' Politely, Rafael pulled out the chair at the end of the veranda table and gestured her to sit down. 'Shall we?'

Sabrina wasn't terribly hungry, but sat anyway. Eating dinner was something to do that wouldn't involve staring at his lithe body until her hands began to shake. Assuming she could even focus on her food with him sitting at the other end of the table, his gaze steady on her face…

'Talking of reminiscences,' Rafael murmured, the ghost of a smile on his lips, 'do you remember those appalling meals at the orphanage? I still have nightmares about that spinach mush they seemed to serve at every other meal.'

'Ah, but we had a different cook at the weekends,' she reminded him. 'I think her name was Iris?' When he nodded, she added, 'Her cooking was at least recognisable as food. It was only weekdays when we got the green slop.'

He laughed. '*Green slop.* Yes, I'd forgotten we called it that.'

The housekeeper reappeared, bearing a tray of silver-lidded dishes, her face impassive as she served the food, poured more champagne into their glasses, and silently withdrew.

'Thankfully, my diet has improved since then,' he

drawled, studying the silver dishes with a sardonic look before raising his glass in a toast. 'To success.'

'To success,' she echoed, sipping her drink with a guarded smile.

Rafael began to eat at once, intent on his meal. Sabrina took a few more nervous gulps of champagne before following suit, her appetite soon revived by freshly shelled crevette prawns served in a fan over a bed of rocket and baby lettuce leaves, a trail of spicy cream dressing adding a piquant note to the dish.

She glanced at him secretively as they ate, finding it hard to connect the powerful, elegant billionaire opposite with the dishevelled tearaway who'd befriended her at the orphanage. Rafael had been a troubled youth, always suggesting some crazy escapade or other. He'd certainly smoothed off his rough edges since then. But she had so many unanswered questions...

By the time she'd finished her spicy prawns and Kyria Diakou had borne the plates away, replacing them with roast lamb served on a bed of fragrant rice, with bread soaked in rosemary oil, the question uppermost in her mind had come back to destroy her appetite.

Why on earth had he demanded she marry him in return for selling her the orphanage?

He'd claimed his having a wife would remedy his playboy reputation with some conservative US company he hoped to do business with. But any presentable woman would have suited his purpose just as well.

'That look on your face... What are you thinking about?' he asked.

She choked on a mouthful of fragrant lamb, glancing up to meet the pair of level near-black eyes staring straight at her, and swallowed carefully. 'Me? Nothing.'

'Hmm…' was his dry rejoinder.

Rafael rose and came loping barefoot towards her, his eyes intent on her face. Sabrina held her breath, watching him. What was he planning? Her gaze was drawn irresistibly to his hard body. The ripple of his pale silk shirt was doing little to conceal the taut six-pack and broad, muscular chest she remembered.

The man was a walking blood pressure spike.

But he merely seized the champagne bottle from the ice bucket and poured more wine expertly into her fluted glass. 'You were running dry.'

'Hardly,' she muttered.

'Sorry?'

'I said, thank you.'

His eyes narrowed on her face, but he refreshed his own glass without comment before returning to his seat.

She gulped down more 'champers', as her father called it, and stared out across the wide blue sea. The rugged cliffs and smooth villa walls glowed with soft golden light as the sun set in the west. The rhythmic click of cicadas in the dry cliffside brush tugged at her—a familiar sound from her childhood. Being back on Calista was like stepping back in time…back into her own troubled past.

Her body was hot and feverish—and not merely because of the heat. She found herself wondering which of the rooms above was his, and whether his bed was as vast and seductively luxurious as her own…

She felt her cheeks heat slowly, much to her embarrassment. Never mind what Rafael was doing... What was *she* doing?

'I hope the guest suite is to your satisfaction.'

His deep voice broke in across her thoughts again.

'It was short notice, but I asked the housekeeper to do her best.'

He hesitated, perhaps taking her silence as a sign that something was wrong.

'Is there anything else you need?'

Her gaze met his with a jolt. She thought of a wave crashing against the dark wall of a harbour and leaping high, its white foam fizzing like the bubbly in her glass.

'No.' She took another sip, felt the heady wine tingling on her tongue. 'The villa is beautiful. And my bedroom is very...well-equipped.'

He raised his eyebrows at her choice of words.

This time she gulped at her wine and choked, unnerved by that intense, unwavering scrutiny.

In fact, she'd been deeply impressed by the guest quarters. His taste was indisputable. The immaculate white walls and huge bed with its ornate dark wood frame and scrolled ends were both opulent and classically simple. Beyond the near-transparent floor-length curtains she'd found a sliding door with discreetly darkened glass that led onto a long stone balcony overlooking the Aegean, its stark lines softened by lush colourful plants spilling at intervals from terracotta urns.

She had stood on that balcony for a long while, staring down into the sparkling turquoise depths, trying to work out why she had agreed to marry him.

It seemed crazy, and not quite real—like something out of a dream.

She had done it primarily to spite her father. To show Andrew Templeton that he might have deceived her and manipulated her for years, but she was no longer his idiot plaything.

But that was not the only reason.

In this moment of supreme turmoil, when all her easy certainties in life had been torn down to reveal the lie that lay behind them, she needed Rafael's constancy.

He was her one still point in a shifting world.

Was it any surprise she had grabbed hold of him to steady herself?

Besides, every time she made the decision to fly back to London and confront her father, she abruptly recalled that Rafael still held the orphanage, and that this marriage was her only way of ensuring it would be saved from demolition.

More than ever she needed to preserve her beloved orphanage. What else did she have in her life that was *real*?

After her bags had been delivered from the mainland that afternoon Sabrina had taken a cooling shower while Thea Diakou had insisted on unpacking her luggage. The marble ensuite bathroom held every possible perfumed shampoo, bath salts, and soap she could possibly want, along with a stack of soft gold-coloured towels.

Cool and clean, she had wandered through the suite afterwards, in the white silk robe discovered on the back of the bathroom door, and found a private sitting room through another door, as expensively furnished as the bedroom, with a deep white leather sofa, a gold ceiling fan quietly whirring overhead, and a display case filled with the most exquisite carved crystal.

Villa Rosa was a far cry from Rafael's dark and twisted roots in the back streets of Calista's main port. Its sumptuous luxury felt decadent, especially compared to their simple lives at the orphanage. And yet this was Rafael's retreat, his place of 'digital detox'. True enough, she had seen no televisions, telephones or computers. And her own electronic devices had failed to find any wireless network.

He was still watching her, and she raised her chin.

'Though I'm going to miss being able to check my emails,' she added, aware of heat in her cheeks. 'Being cut off from the internet and all.'

With a slight smile on his lips, Rafael said, 'It may feel old-fashioned to you, but a more simple way of life suits Villa Rosa. This was a monastery once, you see. The house on the edge of the world, the monks called it.'

'How ironic,' she said without thinking, reaching for her glass again. Goodness, she had nearly polished off the lot. Shrugging, she knocked back the last drop. 'Given you're about as far from a monk as it's possible to get.'

There was silence from the other end of the table.

Oops, she thought, with a barely suppressed hiccup, and put down her glass. *That's torn it.*

Rafael had not expected his childhood soulmate to turn the tables on him so swiftly. He had asked about her room with secret eagerness, hoping she was pleased with what he'd achieved here. It was one of the showpieces of his growing empire, the large and beautiful Villa Rosa, built on the rugged crags above the Aegean. Yet instead of being impressed by his wealth and status she was openly mocking him.

'Given you're about as far from a monk as it's possible to get.'

That was the old Sabrina, laughing as she sharpened her teenage claws on his vulnerable boy's ego. A throwaway jibe, perhaps. All the same, his breath grew shallow as he pondered her words for hidden meaning. She knew of his playboy reputation, of course. But was it possible she was jealous of his past girlfriends?

Once dessert had been offered and declined, Kyria Diakou lit four candles that flickered in milky white containers on the table and began to clear the table. He caught the housekeeper's eye as she removed his plate and she withdrew discreetly, leaving them alone together.

Sabrina was looking out to sea, her chin resting on her hand, her profile even lovelier by candlelight. With all his instincts driving him towards seduction, Rafael felt the distinct press of desire and shifted uncomfortably in his seat, his gaze drawn to the answering flame in Sabrina's eyes.

He had agreed not to touch her. To do so would risk destroying the fledgling trust between them, not to mention endangering his own equilibrium.

Frustration gnawed at him like a physical pain, and he stood abruptly. 'Let's walk down to the sea before bedtime.'

At her look of surprise, he pointed out the low gate at the far end of the veranda.

'The monks carved steps into the cliff, leading down to a diving platform. They're steep, but lit by solar-powered lamps these days. It's perfectly safe.' Seeing her hesitation, he could not resist taunting her. 'Come on, you and I have scaled cliffs together before. Even in the dark.'

'I remember.' There was a glow in her uplifted face.

'Very well, then.' He held out a hand. 'Unless you're afraid?'

Sabrina stood, scraping back her chair. Her eyes flashed blue as summer lightning. 'Show me these steps. I'll go first, if you like.'

One after the other they descended the steps cut deep into the cliff wall. Below them the constant whisper of the Aegean sounded in the dark, its water lapping against rock as it had done for millennia, a warm violet swell in the dusk. The occasional seabird wheeled past their heads. A gentle breeze lifted Sabrina's hair and ruffled the thin fabric of her skirt.

The lower steps were not as deep-set or as well-preserved as the upper ones, and on a narrower part of the descent Sabrina stumbled and lost her footing.

Rafael, whose hand had never been far from her elbow, righted her at once. 'Careful…'

'Thank you,' she muttered, not pulling away from his touch as she had done before.

When they reached the diving platform he pointed out the small alcove in the cliff behind them, which had once housed a religious icon, and the Greek words carved into the smooth stone flags at their feet, left there by the monks.

She studied these with interest, her fair hair shining in the darkness, loose gold strands tumbling across her forehead, hiding her face.

Watching her, he felt his breathing quicken. He longed to brush back her hair, to tilt her face up towards him and set his lips against hers.

Sabrina turned to face him, her blue eyes almost as dark as the Aegean, and put out her hands as though to ward him off. Had she sensed what he was feeling?

Hunger growled inside him. Yes, he'd offered the restriction of a marriage on paper only. And he knew the potential danger she represented to his peace of mind. But the core of his body was molten with desire. Somehow he must turn it back to stone in order to honour their bargain.

It was asking the impossible. Heat gripped him as their eyes met and he began to burn.

'Rafael, no,' she whispered, shaking her head. 'Let's not make a mistake.'

Their eyes clashed, but her lips parted as though in invitation and he felt the warmth of her breath on his skin. Electricity shot through him and he dragged in the warm night air instead, struggling to maintain control.

The temptation to move closer was strong…so strong. To place his mouth on hers and plumb those sweet, hot depths until she moaned in his arms.

'Let's not make a mistake.'

She wasn't immune to their chemistry either. Her whole body told him that without a single word being exchanged. Her wide gaze was fixed on his face, there was a flush in her cheeks, and her chest was heaving as though she were drowning. He almost wanted to laugh, recognising the same symptoms in himself, but there was no amusement left inside him.

They were being whirled away on a dark current, lost to all reason. Had he miscalculated so badly, thinking he could handle her proximity, that a marriage between them was simply a matter of logic trumping desire? Because they had been together only half a day and already his self-control seemed to be deserting him.

Thee mou, he thought hotly. *I have to break this spell.*

Another few seconds and he would be kissing her...

CHAPTER FIVE

BALANCED ON A narrow ledge in the darkness, above the dusky waters of the Aegean, one palm spread wide against the cliff at her back, Sabrina hardly dared breathe. She stared into his eyes and it felt as though time were standing still, locking them both into this endless moment.

The sun had long since dipped below the horizon, yet the island rock behind her was baking to the touch. Its rough, earthy heat reminded her of Rafael. Fierce, fertile, unyielding.

A vision flashed through her head: the two of them in bed together, her thighs locked about his bull-like strength, her softness melting into his volcanic embers.

Champagne was singing in her veins, stripping away her inhibitions. Her cheeks flared with colour as they stared at each other, bodies almost touching, the tension between them sky-high. Frustration gnawed at her as she fought the urge to drag him close by those short, silky strands of hair and press her lips against his.

But even as she weakened and reached for him Rafael straightened, turning his gaze up towards the villa and swearing under his breath in Greek.

Confused, she didn't understand at first what had angered him.

Then she heard it.

Somewhere in the gloom above them a telephone was ringing.

'What the hell?' Sabrina exclaimed. Her own eyes widening in shock, she studied the upturned oval of his face, lit by the solar-powered lamps near the steps. 'I thought you said there was no telephone at the villa?'

Fury flashed through her as she realised he had deliberately prevented her from making contact with the outside world.

'"Digital detox",' she scoffed. '"A more simple way of life." What else have you lied about?'

'I wasn't lying,' he growled, but he was grimacing as he stepped back. 'That's Kyria Diakou's satellite phone. It must be important. Incoming calls are strictly for emergencies only. I'd better go and see who it is.' He held out a hand to help her up the steps. 'You first.'

'I can manage, thanks.'

Stiff with outrage, Sabrina marched to the steps and began climbing. She didn't bother arguing with him. But she was fuming. Always these lies… First her father, now the man she was supposedly about to marry. Was she a liar-magnet?

Her first impulse was to seek out the housekeeper and her satellite phone, call her assistant Shelley and organise a helicopter of her own to whisk her back to England. But by the time she reached the villa, breathing fast, her flush of champagne courage had begun to wear off and she was able to consider the matter more soberly.

He *had* told her about the emergency phone, she recalled. And if she abandoned their arrangement now Rafael would be furious, and might even be inclined towards an act of revenge. She couldn't risk losing her precious orphanage to a bulldozer.

One year.

She just needed to control her impulsive side a little longer—until the novelty of spending time with Rafael had worn off. And that included the almost irresistible urge to tumble into bed with him again.

Having followed Sabrina back to the villa, Rafael waited until she had stamped upstairs to the guest quarters before heading in search of the housekeeper.

'What else have you lied about?'

Frustration churned inside him. Damn that satellite phone. Now Sabrina was angry—and he couldn't blame her.

But part of him was glad she hadn't remembered about Kyria Diakou's phone, nor asked to use it. The fewer people who knew about their arrangement the better.

Sabrina was a high-powered executive, which meant if she was anything like him she must be itching to call her PA and check on the status of her latest deals and companies…perhaps also explain what she was doing on Calista. He didn't doubt her PA's loyalty, but there were ways for calls to be monitored and for information to be leaked out to the highest bidder.

As soon as Templeton heard about their proposed wedding he would doubtless swoop in and try his level best to persuade Sabrina against it. And even though Rafael was determined he would not succeed, she would still be forced into a painful confrontation with her father that she was not ready for. Not so soon after discovering the truth of her parentage.

He could not allow that. She had suffered enough at the hands of that man.

Kyria Diakou was apologetic. 'I'm sorry, sir. I left the phone in the kitchen and the window was open. The call was from your assistant, Linda. She asks you to call her back as soon as possible.'

'Thank you.'

Rafael waited until she had gone before returning Linda's call. It would be late afternoon in New York, he realised, glancing at his watch.

'This had better be good,' he ground out when his PA answered. 'You know how I feel about being disturbed at Villa Rosa.'

'It couldn't be helped,' Linda said hurriedly. She sounded flustered, which was unlike her. 'I thought you should know… Andrew Templeton has been calling your private line all morning. He seems to think you've abducted his daughter.'

'That was quick,' he muttered.

'Sir?'

He heard the shock in her voice and moved quickly to dispel it. 'Miss Templeton is my guest at Villa Rosa and is here of her own accord. That's all you need say if anyone asks.'

He left orders that she was to contact Templeton and let him know Sabrina was safe and would speak to him in the morning, then he rang off.

Furious at Templeton's interference, he stalked out onto the veranda where they'd eaten dinner. The dining table had been stripped of its pristine white cloth and only two flickering candles were still lit, almost burnt down to nothing in their translucent containers. The air was warm, cicadas chirruping fiercely in the darkness.

Rafael stood looking out to sea, even though the dark swell of the Aegean was masked by night. Templeton's accusation was a problem, but not one he hadn't anticipated. The important thing was to keep the billionaire from coming out here to see his daughter in person. Templeton was a clever and cunning manipulator, and Rafael was determined to keep him away from Sabrina for as long as possible. He had no interest in behaving like her protector, but he'd known her long enough to recognise how vulnerable she was feeling right now.

Rafael bent his head and went through the series of breathing exercises taught to him by his therapist years ago, seeking refuge in a state of inner calm.

But inner calm proved elusive. His mind jangled with hot, erotic memories he couldn't shake loose. Her soft lips parting as she stared up at him. The drift of her perfume in the evening air. The rise and fall of her breasts in the figure-hugging midriff top, her flat abdomen just visible below. That tantalising slit in her wraparound skirt, from where a smooth golden-brown thigh had teased him again and again as she'd climbed the steps above him.

His chest expanded and his hands clenched into fists. It was the absolute opposite of calm.

He had nearly lost control tonight and ruined everything with a kiss. Because one kiss would be all it took to crack the foundations of this marriage deal.

The friendship between him and Sabrina ran as deep as the roots of an ancient tree. Everything at the top of the tree was twisted and gnarled with disillusionment, yet below the soil those thick roots still lay tangled together, and they grew limb against limb, merging as one in the trunk. And this shared history was needlessly complicating what ought to be a simple business transaction.

Rafael lifted his head to the fragrant Calistan night and took a deep breath, scenting the air as though preparing himself for battle.

In the past, he'd struggled to feel more than sexual desire for any of the women he'd dated. Several had even accused him of being emotionally cold. But none of them had been friends with him beforehand. Now he needed to channel that bachelor energy into his relationship with Sabrina and stay focused on keeping things professional.

Which was ironic, given they were about to marry…

Sabrina had seen a few wild ponies on Calista as a child, but never ridden one. She had learnt to ride much later, at the exclusive boarding school she'd attended after her adoption had gone through. To sit astride the broad back of a horse, reins in her hands, and control such a vast beast with the mere touch of a heel or the turn of a wrist had been a revelation. Riding had become one of her fa-

vourite pastimes and one at which she'd excelled, both
to her own delight and that of her father, who had en-
couraged her to compete in gymkhanas and other riding
events, where she had even lifted the occasional trophy.

The only disappointment had been how rarely her father had come to watch her compete, after telling her,
'Money doesn't earn itself.' As a child, she'd contented
herself with the hope that one day he would be proud of
her business know-how instead. Now she knew better,
the realisation stung.

Nothing would ever be good enough for that man.
Deep down, Andrew Templeton didn't care about her.
She was an inconvenience, that was all. The child he had
never intended to have but had grudgingly felt he ought
to provide for—especially once his wife had gone and
he'd been able to do so without awkward explanations.

And to think the man had been her hero once. Her
hero!

Tears pricked at her eyes.

Rafael had told her at breakfast about her father's ludicrous accusation that she was being held here against
her will. They'd both agreed she should call him, but be
careful what she said. Yet how on earth could she talk to
him on the phone and not reveal that she knew he was
her biological father?

She was bursting to vent her bitter hurt and grievance
upon the man who had soured the sweetness of her past
with lies. But she knew how to keep a poker face during
negotiations in the boardroom, never letting the opposi-
tion know what she was thinking. Andrew Templeton

himself had taught her that. Now he was about to have those same skills turned on him.

It was a secret pleasure to find that Rafael also knew how to ride. Not merely that, but he seemed born to the saddle, his command of the majestic black beast beneath him stemming from gentle hands and a low, persuasive voice.

Her own horse was also magnificent—a black gelding with a white diamond on his bony forehead and a tendency to shy at gates or unexpected obstacles.

Thankfully, the track they followed was marked as private, and they passed no vehicles to startle either of the horses. Soon leaving Villa Rosa behind, they rode at a brisk trot for about a mile, eventually turning onto a hot, dusty trail with tiered vineyards rising on one side and the sea on the other.

Catching her look, Rafael smiled, throwing her a quizzical glance. 'What have I done to amuse you now?'

'I never figured you for a horseman,' she admitted.

'Doesn't quite fit the profile? Is that it?' His smile hardened into a sneer. 'Low-life street kid…more likely to be seen stealing a horse than riding one.'

There was a distinct snap to his voice.

Her hands tightened on the reins and she drank in a gulp of air, filling her lungs to slow down her automatic urge to counter-accuse.

'I'd forgotten how touchy you are about your background,' she muttered. 'That wasn't what I meant, and you know it.'

'Do I?'

His dark gaze raked her as she sat upright, the reins

gathered in her hands at exactly the correct angle, just as she had been taught.

'My apologies, princess. I don't have the benefit of your expensive education. Everything I know I had to teach myself—here at the library on Calista, and later in Athens. Sometimes I get things wrong.'

Goaded by the sharp note in his voice, Sabrina pressed her heels gently to the horse's flanks and the animal leaped forward in quick response. The easy trot became a canter, and she left Rafael behind in a cloud of dust.

She leant forward over the horse's neck, her fingers twined instinctively in its thick black mane. The wind was in her face and it felt as though she were flying, escaping from the tangle of desire that clouded and confused her mind whenever she and Rafael were together.

But the sweet respite did not last long. Soon she heard a thunder of hooves on the dusty trail at her back, and then he was alongside her, one strong hand grabbing for the bridle.

'Are you mad? Or are you trying to get yourself killed?' he barked as the two horses slowed to a sweating trot and then a sedate walk.

'Oh, stop overreacting. I was never in any danger.' She knocked his hand away from the bridle and eased the horse to a stop herself. 'I'd better phone my father now.'

His dark eyes snapped at her. 'Very well. You'll be careful, though? Because he's a smart man. He'll be listening for signs that you're not telling the truth.'

'I know how to deal with my own father, thanks. Is there a mobile signal here or do we need to keep riding?'

He levelled a glare at her that spoke of his frustration, but gave a terse shrug. 'We've gone far enough now. You should be able to make the call.'

He hesitated, leaning forward to pat his horse's shiny neck as the animal snorted and breathed heavily beneath him.

'Look, I'm sorry about what I said back there. You didn't choose someone so privileged to be your father.' Narrow-eyed, he studied her flushed face. 'Before you make this call, I hope you haven't changed your mind about our deal. The paperwork's all in motion—there's no turning back.'

'I haven't changed my mind,' she snapped, still annoyed by how he'd wrongly assumed her horse had run away with her.

In some ways Rafael reminded her of her father, who had insisted she should operate independently of his wealth and influence, yet would still sweep in at the first sign of trouble to 'rescue' her.

Gathering the reins, Sabrina dismounted and looped them over a nearby fence pole. Then she fished her mobile from her pocket, walked a few paces out of earshot and turned it on, keeping her back to Rafael.

The screen displayed several signal bars and a dozen anxious messages popped up from her father, all chiming at once. She skim-read the texts before calling him back, hands trembling as she primed herself for a difficult conversation.

Her father answered almost immediately. 'Sabrina, thank God. Where on earth are you?'

Without waiting to hear a reply, Andrew Templeton pressed on, an explosive mix of fear and fury ticking behind every word.

'I received the most insolent message last night from that thug Rafael Romano. Are you okay? Has he hurt you?' He snatched a breath before exclaiming, 'I swear, if he's touched so much as a hair on your head I'll kill him with my bare hands!'

Every fibre of her being wanted to scream defiance at him, yet somehow Sabrina heard herself say coolly, 'Calm down, Dad. I'm fine.'

'Are you?' Templeton sounded frustrated, and more than a little suspicious. 'When we spoke yesterday you said you were on Calista and your mobile was playing up. I couldn't get hold of you again. So I notified the local police that you were missing.'

'You did *what*?'

'What else did you expect? If you've been trying to give me a heart attack, I congratulate you on nearly achieving it.'

That had to be his usual dramatic hyperbole. But she felt a flutter of anxiety. However badly he had behaved towards her, he was still her father.

'Dad, please tell me you're joking.'

'Not entirely. I've been out of my mind with worry. Your hire car was returned by an unknown third party. The hotel where you'd been staying claimed you'd checked out by phone and asked for your luggage to be collected—also by some unknown person. Then I learnt you've been travelling solo instead of with your team. All major red flags.' He was breathing heavily. 'Do you have *any* idea how much you're worth, sweetheart? You're a kidnapper's dream.'

'Yes, but I still can't believe you called the police without even waiting twenty-four hours.'

Sabrina took a few deep breaths, reminding herself to keep a tight lid on her emotions. Besides, it wouldn't do any good to yell at him. The man was as stubborn as an ox.

'I'm not an idiot. I didn't want anyone to know I was on Calista. The publicity might have derailed the deal I was trying to broker. That's why I was travelling unaccompanied.'

'It only takes one person to kidnap you, Sabrina,' her father pointed out. 'I did some digging to find out what exactly you were doing there. I even spoke to that ditzy assistant of yours—'

'You spoke to Shelley?' Her voice was a squeak of dismay. Her assistant was terrified of Andrew Templeton and would never have been able to withstand one of his trademark interrogations.

'Yes, and she eventually admitted you'd arranged a meeting with Rafael Romano, of all people.' He expelled a noisy breath, his voice grating with disapproval. 'You can imagine my reaction. I got on the phone to his people at once, but nobody seemed to know where he was. Finally, I got a call in the early hours, letting me know you were safe and spending a few days with Romano on Calista.'

She closed her eyes at the suddenly dangerous note in his voice.

'Darling, you need to come home straight away. I haven't forgotten the state you were in after Paris.'

She counted to five before replying, suppressing the words in her head. Words of anger and disillusion that would expose what she knew about him.

'Dad, please…'

It still irked her that, unbeknownst to her, Andrew Templeton had been secretly monitoring her movements during the Paris trip. On her return home to England, the humiliation of her father's lecture on one-night stands had been one of the most cringe-worthy experiences of her life. She had thought it embarrassing, but also rather endearing that he cared enough to keep an eye on her like that. Now it merely underlined how possessive and controlling he was over everyone in his life, and her fury grew.

She turned, shooting a wary glance over her shoulder, to see that Rafael had also dismounted and was close by, his gaze intent on her face. Could he hear what was being said?

'Look,' she muttered grittily into the phone, 'I can't talk right now. There's something I need to think about, so I'm going off-grid for a few days. I'll call you after the weekend.'

'Is Romano there with you now? Is he the reason you're going "off-grid"—whatever the hell *that's* supposed to mean.'

She swallowed, hot-cheeked. 'He's an old friend and he's been supporting me through some issues, that's all.'

'Romano was more than a friend once, though, wasn't he? I haven't forgotten.'

'I have to ring off now.'

'Sabrina, wait—' he began, but she interrupted him.

'This is my business, Dad, not yours. Please don't ring Shelley and frighten her again. I can't afford to lose her—she's an excellent assistant.'

'Fine, but at least let me help.'

Her father seemed to be almost pleading with her. That shocked her… It was so out of character. But it also made her suspicious.

'Whatever you're facing, tell me what these "issues" are and I'll sort them out for you.'

He was shifting tactics, trying to probe her for weak spots.

'I'm sorry, Daddy,' she insisted. 'Not this time. This is something I have to do on my own. I'll be in touch as soon as possible, I promise.'

She ended the call while he was still protesting, and hurriedly turned off the phone before he could ring her back. Then she looked up to find Rafael still watching her, his hands in his pockets, his face expressionless. But she sensed what he was feeling, all the same. Satisfaction that his plan was still working—that she hadn't betrayed him and they would soon be man and wife. But also irritation.

Fury whipped through her—a fury she had wanted to direct towards her father but hadn't been able to. 'Well? Spit it out. Whatever you're thinking.'

'Going "off-grid" to think about something?' he said, his brows raised. 'As cover stories go, that's a bit weak.

Anyone would think you wanted *Daddy* to come and find you.'

'Don't use that word,' she snapped.

'You did.'

'Only because I didn't want him to think anything was wrong.'

'I'm not sure you did a great job. But let's hope I'm mistaken.'

Unlooping its reins from the post, Rafael brought the black gelding towards her, his gaze lifted to the deep blue skies above.

'The sun's getting high. We should probably think about turning back.'

She mounted the horse with easy skill, ignoring his proffered hand. 'I thought there was *"no turning back"*?' she pointed out, quoting what he'd said earlier.

He said nothing to this jibe, merely mounting his own horse. Soon they were both thundering back along the track to Villa Rosa, side by side in the dusty sunshine.

The day felt curiously the same. Light glittered on the blue Aegean exactly as it had done before. Calista looked as wild and beautiful as ever. Yet something had shifted between them during that brief phone call to her father. She'd pushed past her inner misgivings to accept their marriage as a done deal, and seen triumph flare in Rafael's eyes as he'd noted and understood that change.

Let him gloat, she thought, her mouth compressing as she brooded over that call to her father. This would still be a marriage on her own terms, not Rafael's. She'd made that clear from the start. His ring on her finger, the orphanage deeds in her possession, her father's control left behind. No more, no less.

So what was this fluttering dread in the pit of her stomach? Why did she feel as though she'd broken free from one over-protective male only to weld herself to another?

CHAPTER SIX

THE COMPLEX MULTI-PAGE contract Rafael had instructed to be drawn up for their one-year marriage was brought over by his local lawyer, Christopoulos, along with a date and time for their wedding. Among its many clauses was a stipulation that Sabrina must attend a minimum of three high-profile social events as his wife over the course of the year, with the first coming up soon, its details highlighted so she could make a note in her diary.

He saw her eyes widen as she read through the document. The named event was the annual charity ball in Paris where they had met five years ago.

'Everything all right?' he asked, his jaw clenched, wondering if she was about to renege on their agreement.

But Sabrina replied, 'Perfectly,' with total composure as she accepted a pen from Christopoulos.

She signed her name at the bottom of the last page with no change of expression, but Rafael felt his own heart jerk as he took the pen from her. Still, he signed his name with a flourish before handing the contract back to Christopoulos, convincing himself that he was doing the right thing.

This bloodless union might frustrate him, but it should cure him of his obsession with Sabrina. After that, he could finally begin to live his life…

'Congratulations,' the lawyer told them, shaking hands with them. 'You may rely on my discretion, Mr Romano.'

On the morning of their wedding they took a speedboat out from the jetty below the villa, accompanied by Kyria and Kyrios Diakou, who had enthusiastically agreed to be their witnesses. It seemed his housekeeper and her husband believed this to be a love match, for they kept smiling at him and Sabrina with undisguised approval.

Sabrina herself had taken his breath away on emerging from her room that morning. She was wearing an off-the-peg wedding dress bought in Athens on a quick helicopter trip yesterday. An up-and-coming Greek designer had created a gown which would have been dismissed by most of the glamorous, high-maintenance women he'd dated in recent years, their tastes being more exorbitantly expensive. On Sabrina, though, it looked a million dollars. Its ruched bodice cupped her breasts with delicate ivory silk; spaghetti shoulder straps exposed sun-kissed skin. The frou-frou skirts of layered tulle ended just above the knee, displaying an expanse of thigh as he helped her into the speedboat.

Arousal taunted him, and his heart beat a little faster as he imagined what delightful silky scraps of lingerie she might be wearing underneath… Seconds later he was slapping himself down for even allowing his thoughts to wander in such a dangerous direction. This would be no ordinary marriage and he needed it to remain platonic.

'Get a grip…' he muttered.

'Sorry?' Sabrina looked round at him with wide blue eyes.

'I said, you might want to hold on to something.' He planted himself in front of the speedboat wheel, running through the engine checks. As his bride found a seat and gripped the side rail he glanced at Thea and Nikos. 'Ready?'

Kyria Diakou smiled up at him, her arms bristling with fragrant floral arrangements, all white roses and spreading greenery. Her husband was beside her, distinctly uncomfortable in formal wear. 'Ready, sir.'

The speedboat trip did not take long. His luxury superyacht had been sailed from Piraeus and was now anchored out in the deeper waters between islands, swaying slightly in the sea breeze. The hull gleamed white in the sunlight, chrome rails glinting, and the whole crew was assembled on deck and standing to attention as they boarded the vessel.

'Welcome aboard, Mr Romano,' the captain said, saluting him before bowing slightly to Sabrina. 'Miss Templeton. Congratulations.'

'Thank you,' Sabrina said, smiling warmly.

Rafael caught her eye, a smile tugging at his own lips. He was remembering a time when the two of them had watched a Calistan wedding party assemble for photographs with the picturesque harbour as a backdrop. A couple of urchins themselves, they had mocked the bride in her finery and the groom in his stiff, formal clothes, never guessing they might one day be marrying each other.

Even now he couldn't quite believe it.

Him and Sabrina…

No, it couldn't be. She had always been too good for him. Her warmth and generosity, the sparkling beauty in her eyes… How could a boy from the backstreets reach for such a star? It would burn his fingers to the bone.

And yet here they were.

'This way, if you please.'

The captain led them to a beautifully constructed wedding area on the open deck, laid out with deep red carpets, white floral arrangements in high urns, and chairs for the crew, witnesses and select members of the world's press, who were already gathered, watching in excitement for their first glimpse of the happy couple.

'Miss Templeton, over here!', one of the photographers shouted.

Sabrina turned that way, an apprehensive look on her face, as the woman climbed on a chair to take a shot of the two of them together, standing arm in arm, with the smooth Aegean a blue haze behind them.

He could see why the few press they'd invited were lapping this up. Sabrina's blonde hair had been dressed with flowers, and long burnished gold strands trailed delightfully over her shoulders and down her back. She looked more like a wood nymph, one of the dryads of Ancient Greece, than the hard-headed businesswoman he knew her to be. The perfect image for some glossy socialite gossip piece or wedding column.

Rafael smiled down at her while more pre-wedding

photographs were taken. 'You look radiant,' he murmured, and brushed her cheek with one knuckle. 'Smile more. Your father will be studying these pictures with a magnifying glass, remember?'

'You don't need to tell me that,' she responded, but turned a smiling face towards his. 'You look…um…very handsome in that tux.'

His brows flicked up. 'What? This old thing?'

Sabrina gurgled with genuine laughter, and on impulse he snaked an arm about her waist, drawing her towards him as though for a kiss. The photographers went crazy, snapping candid shots and shouting out impertinent instructions as he stared down into the turbulent blue depths of Sabrina's eyes, their mouths bare inches apart.

Her laughter died away, and her lips parted as if in shock. She whispered, 'Erm…does this need to be quite so realistic?'

Her gaze locked with his, her tulle skirt rustling against him, and everything about her felt maddeningly feminine.

'It's important to put on a show,' he reminded her, his voice unsteady, but he released her, turning to the waiting minister. 'Shall we do this?'

The ceremony seemed to fly by. The sun beat down on them, and those watching murmured a sigh of appreciation when the minister asked for any objections to be aired and none were. The deck rocked gently beneath them as they exchanged vows in soft voices that nonetheless seemed to carry across the water, for even passengers on passing vessels applauded and called out congratulations.

Rafael kept smiling throughout, keeping up the charade for the paparazzi, but he wasn't as calm and controlled as he'd expected to be today. Quite the opposite, in fact. His chest felt tight and his heart was thumping so loudly he was sure everyone on deck could hear it.

Meanwhile Sabrina never lost her poise, repeating the minister's words on cue, no hint of uncertainty in her voice. Rafael had to admire her single-minded focus—especially given how much she valued her independence. Sabrina punched through the day, her eyes on the prize, and did not even flinch when he pushed a heavy gold band onto her finger—the wedding ring that had arrived only that morning, express couriered from Cartier in Paris.

Finally, it was done, and they were man and wife.

'You may kiss the bride, if you wish,' the minister said, beaming at them.

The photographers shifted, hurriedly leaving their seats and scrambling for a better view of the married couple. Rafael felt the irritation of their presence, but accepted the necessity of having at least a few of the world's media here.

It was no good their marrying in secret, after all. He had to signal to the world that he was now a respectable married man. And she wanted her father to know about it too.

As Sabrina lifted her face towards him, dutifully playing the role of newly wedded bride, Rafael looked down at her with a sudden stab of trepidation. This would be their first kiss since Paris, and already his nerves were flaring up, memory kicking him back to the morning after...

'Rafael...?' she murmured, faint surprise in her face.

Frustrated by his own weakness, he bent his head and kissed his bride.

Thee mou!

At the touch of his lips to hers his heart rate rocketed, his body instantly aroused, blood pumping to every extremity. His senses spun and drowned him. He was overwhelmed by her warmth, her curves, the light fragrance of the flowers in her hair. It was all he could do not to drag her against him like a sex-starved caveman and slot his mouth firmly against hers, plundering her sweetness until she could no longer stand...

But they were in public. In full view of the yacht's crew—not to mention those members of the press, whose laughter and amused whistles brought him back to his senses.

Stunned, he straightened slowly, his hands releasing her, and saw the same shock in her dazed blue eyes.

It felt surreal to be married to his childhood friend, he thought, forcing a smile back to his lips. Like waking from the strangest dream to find it reality...

Back at Villa Rosa, he gave the Diakous the evening off, insisting he would himself serve the cold supper which his housekeeper had already prepared and left in the fridge on his command. The couple only lived a short distance away, in the villa grounds, in a self-contained annex. But he wished to guarantee that he and Sabrina would be alone together that evening, even if their marriage was destined not to be consummated.

'We're leaving now for our honeymoon on Paradiso, my island in the Caribbean,' he had blithely lied to the carefully selected group of reporters after the ceremony. 'We're delighted and honoured that you could share our special day with us,' he had said, linking hands with Sabrina. 'Aren't we, Sabbie?'

When she'd nodded, he had kissed her hand and turned back to them with a pleading smile.

'All we ask is a little privacy for the next few weeks while we settle into married life together. Thank you.' He had led his new wife back towards the waiting speedboat. 'Feel free to enjoy the champagne and canapés for as long as you like before leaving. My on-board chef is *excellent*.'

The paps had shouted questions after them, Sabrina in particular, but she had already said she would not speak to the press, only pose for photographs.

'I'm not shy,' she'd explained to him beforehand, 'I'm just not terribly good at dodging questions.'

'That's because you're an honest soul,' he'd told her, and meant it.

Now they were safely back at their real honeymoon destination he took a moment in the gatehouse, to check the camera array and the perimeter alarms that kept them safe from intruders. He needed to be sure none of the paparazzi had found a way to follow them after they'd left the yacht, perhaps stealthily by drone.

But everything was quiet and still outside, only the cicadas chirping in the sunny warmth of the early evening.

Satisfied that the villa was secure, he followed Sabrina into the cool, air-conditioned interior and stood watching as she removed the headdress of flowers the hairdresser had arranged for her earlier that morning.

'Shall I pour us a drink?' he asked, thrown off balance by how silent the house was without his housekeeper. His nerves felt raw and unsteady.

'Yes, why not?' she said, her voice unnaturally high, and then kicked off her shoes before running upstairs. 'I…I'm going to change.'

Rafael hesitated, and then followed more slowly, heading for the sanctuary of his own suite. There, he changed out of his formal dark suit and tie into shorts and a crisp white T-shirt. Barbed thoughts and volatile emotions kept intruding into the orderly calm of his bedroom and he pushed them away, even stepping out on the balcony at one stage to meditate on the sea and breathe deep, struggling to regain control.

He wanted tonight to be special, but not as it would be for most married couples. More an outward symbol of how their marriage would work—calmly, and with the gentle affection of old friends who were gaining mutual satisfaction from an arrangement that would further their plans and ambitions.

Back in the bedroom, he fetched the deeds to the orphanage and a small, brightly wrapped gift from his bedside cabinet. The gift he turned over in his hand, unsure what to do with it, before slipping it into his pocket. He would see how the evening went.

Barefoot, he was about to head downstairs again

when he heard a tiny, breathless noise from Sabrina's bedroom suite.

He stopped on the top stair, breathing harshly through gritted teeth, one hand gripping the banister until his knuckles showed white. He had heard that noise often enough as a child not to recognise it now...

It was the sound of a woman struggling not to cry.

Not since waking up in hospital the day after the car crash that had killed her mother had Sabrina been so unhappy.

Then, it had been the horrific discovery that her beloved mum was dead, and she would never hug her or speak to her again, while she herself had been left orphaned and disfigured, with no idea who her father was nor if she had any living relatives at all.

Now, uppermost in her head was the fear that she had made a terrible mistake, and one from which she might never recover. In punishing her father for his perfidy, had she merely punished herself?

She had told herself that securing the orphanage was all that mattered. Now Rafael's ring was on her finger and she was no longer Miss Templeton but Mrs Romano, with all that implied. Too late, the magnitude of what she'd done struck her.

While she might only have one year in which to endure this loveless marriage, she could not walk away without the deeds to the orphanage. But they had been married several hours and he had not mentioned their bargain yet.

What if he *never* handed her the deeds?

What if she had missed a legal hitch in the contract, for instance? Some carefully worded clause in the small print that would prevent her from ever owning the orphanage?

She had seen that tactic in business deals too often not to know how long a legal wrangle over the wording of a contract might drag on. Not simply months, but years… Long past the stated period of their marriage, in other words.

Sabrina stared at herself in the full-length mirror. The unhappiest bride in the world looked back at her, a perfect snapshot in ivory silk, but with both hands clasped to her cheeks, tears spilling from red-rimmed eyes. Still, she gritted her teeth and held back her sobs, too proud to let him hear her misery.

A creak as the door opened brought her around, rigid with embarrassment. Wiping her face with her hands, she glared at her new husband, framed in the doorway.

Rafael had changed into casual clothes, and was no longer the austere stranger who had stood by her side throughout their perfunctory wedding service. Yet he was also unrecognisable as the rebellious, weed-tall youth she had grown up with. That boy would have understood her pain and rushed to comfort her—not looked back at her so blankly.

She could barely recall speaking her vows today. Yet she must have done so, for here they were—married. The heavy gold band on her finger proved it.

What she did remember was his kiss.

It had been Paris all over again. Pure molten electricity, flashing from her lips to her core in three seconds flat. How did he *do* that? Her shoulders had been warm and tingly from his touch long after he'd released her, and there had been a memory in her head, spinning round and round like a glitterball, of her and Rafe in bed together, making love. As her eyes had opened they'd met those dark depths and she'd known she was tempted to repeat the same mistake…

'I didn't hear you knock,' she snapped, thrusting her hand with its incriminating glitter of gold behind her back.

Rafael's gaze narrowed on her face. 'You've been crying. Why?'

'Brides always cry on their wedding day—didn't you know that?' She had been trying for matter-of-fact but it came out flippant. The shake in her voice didn't help. 'It's tradition.'

He came further into the room, searching her face. He was barefoot again, and in shorts, his legs lean and muscular, with a dusting of dark hair.

'I told you. I need my privacy—' she began fiercely, but then she saw he held out a large envelope.

'Here,' he said, his gaze unreadable. 'The deeds to the orphanage, made out in your name. Now you're free to do whatever you want with the place.' He took a step back as she took the envelope. 'A deal's a deal.'

'Oh.'

She had misjudged him.

'Thank you,' she whispered, and opened the envelope, peeking inside to see a wodge of legal documents and associated papers. Her heart flipped as she realised

what this meant. The orphanage would no longer be demolished. 'That's… That's wonderful.'

Sadly, her memories of the place were tainted now,
by what she'd learned about her father. But at least Rafael had kept his word.

Hesitantly, he drew a small gift-wrapped object from
his pocket and held that out to her too. 'A wedding gift.'

Stunned into silence, Sabrina stared at his expressionless face, and then at the gift resting on his open
palm. 'For…? For me?'

Inhaling sharply, she dropped the envelope on the
bed, scrubbed at her damp cheeks again, and took a few
tentative steps towards him.

'I didn't get you anything, I'm sorry.'

He said nothing, merely waited.

Scooping the gift from his palm, she tore off the taste-
ful gift wrap and found a tiny blue-white crystal dolphin
inside the package, its smooth body arched in flight.
Gasping in delight, Sabrina ran a fingertip appreciatively
over its cool, delicate shape. The detail was exquisite,
right down to its intelligent, gleaming eyes.

'Oh, Rafe, how lovely!' She closed her hand over the
glass dolphin, warmth rushing to her heart. 'Thank you.'

He had been holding himself tense, but seemed to
relax at this, his lips curving in a rare smile. 'I thought
you'd like it. You always loved dolphins as a girl. You
remember how we used to lie on the cliffs and watch
them leaping in the bay?'

She nodded.

'I found that one on a market stall at the port. It's not
worth much, but—'

'It's perfect.'

Rafael inclined his head, and she sensed pleasure in the brief gesture. 'Now, why were you crying? And don't try to deflect the question this time.' His jaw tensed. 'I thought you were happy to marry me. Have you changed your mind?'

Carefully, she turned to place the crystal dolphin on her dressing table, next to her make-up case and bottles of perfume. 'Of course I'm happy.'

'You don't look it.' His voice vibrated with tangled emotions.

She lifted her gaze to his face, trying to guess what he was thinking, but it was impossible. She hated that. Rafael was a closed door to her now, when once they had been able to read each other's thoughts freely. The loss of that intimacy pierced her heart, like steel thrust deep into her chest. Where had their friendship gone?

Another hot tear crept over the brim of one eyelid and rolled down her cheek. She turned her head and rubbed it away with her fist, hoping he hadn't noticed.

'Sabrina…' His voice was husky.

'I'm fine,' she insisted, and flashed him a bright, false smile. 'It's been a long day, that's all. And I was worried my father might suddenly turn up and—'

'You don't need to fear him ever again,' he interrupted her. 'You're my wife now. He can't touch you.'

She lowered her gaze, surprised by the protective look in his eyes. 'It was so hot at the wedding too. Remind me never to get married on a yacht again.'

It was meant as a joke, but he didn't smile.

'I'm dying of thirst,' she finished plaintively.

'That, at least, is easily remedied. I asked Kyria Diakou to leave a bottle of champagne on ice. I'll go down and pour us a glass each.'

He hesitated, studying her. Something in her core awoke at the look in his eyes. Awoke and began to thaw rapidly, leaving her body humming with need.

'You really do look stunning in that dress,' he said. 'Every man on that yacht was staring at you. No doubt wishing he was the one marrying you.'

'Thank you.'

Her heart stuttered at the deep note in his voice, but she kept smiling, holding herself still with an effort.

'Now that we're home, though,' she added, realising with a start how soon she had come to think of Villa Rosa as 'home', 'I'd better slip into something cooler.'

This was not merely her excuse for having run up-stairs on arriving. The wedding dress was fitted, and sat snugly about her breasts and hips—too tight for these long, Calistan summer evenings.

'I came up here to change and then got sidetracked.'

'Of course. Excuse me.'

He turned as though to leave her alone to change, but some devil made her call him back.

'Actually, I…I could do with a hand,' she burst out, and felt a rush of heat to her cheeks as he glanced back at her, dark brows raised. 'There's a tricky zip…'

Half of her expected him to see the bait and walk away. They had both signed that no-sex contract, after all. But that didn't mean she wasn't interested in him physically. Much to her hot-cheeked embarrassment…

Only he didn't say no.

'In that case, you'd better allow me.'

He walked towards her as she stood frozen in place and turned her gently to face the full-length mirror. His hands were warm on her shoulders. Staring into the mirror, she tried but couldn't read the expression in his eyes, shielded by long thick lashes.

'Ah, I see there's a hook…'

She held her breath as his fingers moved over her back, gently unfastening the top of her dress.

'And there's the "tricky zip"…'

As the zip was released, the dress sagged in a rustle of white silk, and she grabbed at the bodice to keep it in place, her heart thumping. Her mouth was dry—and not simply through the thirst she'd claimed.

Their eyes met in the mirror.

'Sabrina…' he whispered.

Electricity leapt between them like wildfire, just as it had done when he'd kissed her after the wedding ceremony. She heard the fierce intake of his breath as his hands moved to the thin spaghetti straps of her dress, slipping them off her shoulders, his fingers caressing her delicately. She turned, gazing up into his lean, dark face, her whole body aching. Her palms were damp, her breathing ragged.

What were they doing?

There was silence between them as their gazes locked.

Heat rushed to her core and she could have moaned out loud. Her whole body was tingling with excitement as she waited for his kiss.

But Rafael surprised her by releasing her and stepping back carefully. 'Maybe that champagne would be a good idea.'

'Um…okay, yeah.' Embarrassed, she swallowed hard, fighting for self-control against an inner tide of longing, all her nerves prickling and vibrant. 'You go. I'll be down in a minute,' she added, and even managed a fleeting smile. 'Thanks for your help with the dress.'

To her relief he didn't comment, but merely gave a nod and left the room. Hearing him go downstairs, Sabrina kicked the bedroom door shut, stepped out of the sensuous pool of silk and tulle, and sank onto the bed in bra and panties, shaking with reaction. Blood was rushing in her veins, its turbulent beat almost deafening.

What was wrong with her?

Enticing an experienced playboy like Rafael to get so close was asking for the kind of trouble she was ill-equipped to handle. She had slept with him once, yes. But she was still little more than an innocent when it came to sex. All she knew was that her breasts felt heavy and full, and heat was throbbing between her legs as she imagined him removing the wedding dress fully and lying down with her on this bed, like any other couple on their wedding day…

Her wide-eyed gaze met her own flushed reflection in the mirror, then dropped to his unexpected wedding gift—the crystal dolphin. Its blue-white glassy body leapt perpetually, like her heart, taking joy in this tiny Greek island.

He might have spotted the dolphin on a market stall in passing, but there had been nothing random about his choice. It was a gift that spoke to her deeply—not merely a reminder of her childhood here on Calista, but of what they had been to each other back then.

She could still taste the magic of their time together on this bee-rich island, with its cliffs swathed in rosemary, sage and purple-coloured thyme, where they had once lain on rocks together to watch dolphins at play in the glittering aquamarine waters. Simpler times…when their friendship had meant everything to each other.

Had those days gone for ever, or was it possible to get them back?

CHAPTER SEVEN

RAFAEL STRETCHED AND rolled over in the morning light, nude in the tangled sheets, covering his eyes with his forearm.

He was a married man. His new bride had eaten her dinner last night in a meek silence, eyes downcast, before retiring to bed without him.

He could have gone after her. Instead, he had kept to the contract and sat on the veranda long into the early hours, drinking whisky and staring out at the violet mass of the Aegean, breathing in the hot, dusty night air of Calista, his birthplace and spiritual home. Because he had known he dared not touch her. The risk to his sanity would be too great.

A tiny sound had him scrambling up in bed, abruptly aware that he was not alone in the bedroom.

Sabrina was slumped in an easy chair near his bed, wearing a short, flimsy nightdress that left little to the imagination, bare legs curled beneath her, eyes closed. Her blonde head was resting on her shoulder while her chest rose and fell gently under a delicate white lace and satin bodice.

Baffled, he threw back the covers, and she stirred, opening her eyes to peer sleepily across at him. Then he saw her blue gaze widen and her body stiffen as she realised he was naked.

'Good morning,' he said with heavy irony, making a swift grab for his shorts. 'Forgive the floor show. But what the hell are you doing in my bedroom?'

Red-cheeked, Sabrina stumbled to her feet and fled back to her own room without a word.

'Sabrina?' he called after her, but she didn't come back.

Astonished, Rafael stood beside the bed for a moment, racking his brains for a reason why she should have chosen to sleep on a chair in his room on their wedding night. Then he shrugged it away. No doubt once she'd woken up fully she would feel able to tell him.

Since he was unlikely to get back to sleep, he showered briskly to shake off his hangover before selecting an outfit to wear. But when he went to knock at Sabrina's door later he found her suite empty.

Downstairs, Kyria Diakou appeared on the veranda with a shy smile and a tray of fresh fruit and yoghurt. 'Breakfast, sir?'

'Only coffee today, thank you.' Wincing, he drew on reflective sunglasses against the morning glare. 'Have you seen my wife?'

'Why, yes, sir.' His housekeeper put down the tray and pointed to the pool below. 'Kyria Romano said she wished to swim before breakfast.'

Glancing that way with feigned nonchalance, he saw a sleek blonde head bobbing in the water. Sabrina was swimming lengths of the pool in a breaststroke, her rhythm swift but steady, the slender line of her body graceful as ever.

The housekeeper excused herself, saying she was going to fetch fresh coffee for him.

Rafael got up and sauntered down the steps to the pool. There was a towel over one of the loungers, and a pot of coffee with a solitary cup set on a low table.

Walking to the poolside, he waited for Sabrina to return to that end. She was doing a front crawl now, low in the water, her movements more aggressive than before, though the splash was minimal and her technique super-efficient. Even through the distorting ripple of water he could see the lush swell of her breasts captured in a white bikini top, and was glad of his sunglasses masking his stare.

Reaching the wall of the pool, Sabrina stopped dead, gasping as she stared up at him, blue eyes wide with surprise. Blonde tendrils of hair stuck to her forehead and cheeks and she had no make-up on, her face beautifully natural.

'Oh!'

'Hello, again.'

His gaze dipped to the deep shadow between her breasts in the clinging white bikini and his arousal grew, suddenly urgent and uncomfortable.

Acting purely on instinct, he smiled as her gaze tangled with his. 'The pool looks refreshing in this heat. I'll join you, if I may.'

Before she could protest, he stripped off his white T-shirt, discarding it on the nearest lounger. Without a word, she swam slowly backwards, watching with an almost shocked expression as he drew off loose-fitting trousers to reveal a pair of black swimming trunks underneath.

Rafael dived in past her, cutting through the cool water for several meters before surfacing almost at the other end of the infinity pool. Shaking back his wet hair, he swam towards her, his arousal undiminished. In fact, the glimpse he'd enjoyed of her bare legs and midriff under the water had inflamed his desire.

'I'm sorry about earlier,' she volunteered. 'I…I heard you having a nightmare just before dawn, so I woke you and stayed with you a while.' She trod water, breathing fast, her eyes locked on his face. 'I only meant to sit there a few minutes. I must have dropped off to sleep.'

'A nightmare?' He frowned, made uncomfortable by the thought. 'I don't remember you waking me up. Did I speak to you?'

'Not really… You went straight back to sleep.'

There were dark shadows under her eyes; he studied them, frowning. 'I'm sorry if I disturbed you.'

'No, it's fine,' she said quickly. 'I was awake anyway… reading a book.' She licked her lips. 'I couldn't sleep. Too much champagne yesterday.'

Years ago, he had once shared a hotel room with a colleague on a team-building exercise. He'd told him the next day that he'd shouted out during his sleep. It had thrown him off balance, being made aware that he suffered bad dreams, and he wondered what embarrassing words he might have uttered while unconscious.

'Did I make a noise? Say something?'

When Sabrina hesitated, he moved closer. He couldn't help himself. It was as though an invisible cord was tugging them together.

'Tell me what I said.'

He could smell her light perfume even in the water. Her sleek hair hung wet about her face, and her delicate eyelashes were beaded with tiny jewels of water that shone and sparkled in the sunlight. Erotic fantasies chased through his mind even while he struggled to keep his thoughts out of his face.

No, not fantasies.

Memories of their night together in Paris…

He had known in advance that she would be at the charity ball. He'd considered backing out of the event at first, but his curiosity, once piqued, had got the better of him.

That first glance of her in Paris had shocked him to the core. He'd seen photographs, of course. Even a few short videos. Sabrina Templeton had been everywhere on social media that year, as one of the youngest winners ever of a prestigious award for women in business. Yet he'd somehow convinced himself that how Sabrina looked on screen was not how she looked in real life. That the photographs and videos must have been touched up.

Because the Sabrina he'd known as a kid had been a completely different girl. Blonde hair, yes. But the flawless skin, the perfect make-up, the elegance and poise… All those belonged to a stranger.

Having worked through his disbelief at her appearance, Rafael had set out to get close to her. He'd never intended to seduce her—only to see how much of the old Sabrina was left under the expensive packaging.

But the bittersweet nostalgia of dancing and drinking champagne with the girl he'd known when they were both barefoot urchins in the dusty backstreets of Calista had drugged his senses, and before the night was out he'd suggested a nightcap at her nearby hotel.

It was the first time they'd been alone for years. The first time as adults. When he'd kissed her, unable to resist, her response had electrified him. Sabrina had been so eager, so willing, her passion naked and spontaneous, and he had allowed himself to be swept away...

Waking in her bed the next morning, he'd experienced an emotion he had only felt once before—the day Andrew Templeton had come to collect her from the orphanage.

Fear.

As a boy, he had not known that emotion for what it was. But that morning in Paris, seeing Sabrina's head on the pillow next to him, Rafael had recognised the stomach-churning emotion and recoiled from it. He had felt much the same terror when trying to protect his mother from his father—and failing abysmally.

Fear had gripped him as he'd stared at Sabrina's sleeping face. The fear of loss and inadequacy for the second time in his life.

Silently, he'd pulled on his clothes and left her lying there, still blissfully asleep, unaware of the turmoil in his heart.

Sabrina had called him later, shy and confused, asking where he'd gone and why he'd left without a word.

Caught off guard, Rafael had said a few things he hadn't meant, and had known from the silence on the other end of the phone line that he'd hurt her deeply.

Better that, though, than have to live with his failure again. Because he wasn't perfect. One day he would disappoint her, or not be there for her when she needed him. One day he would fail her as he had failed his mother. And that awareness of his own inadequacy was too much to bear.

After Paris, he had vowed never to see Sabrina again. But then he'd managed to acquire the orphanage on Calista. And, hunting through its records one day, looking for details on another friend who'd been adopted and whom he'd wished to trace, he had stumbled across a dusty old folder of documents relating to Sabrina's arrival at the orphanage and her later adoption—records which had never been computerised, perhaps deliberately.

At first he had not understood what he was looking at, it had seemed so fantastical. Then, slowly, the truth had dawned on him.

Fury and disbelief pouring through him like acid, he had paced the deserted orphanage, cursing and smashing his fist repeatedly into the walls. But the person he had really wanted to hurt—the villain of the piece—had not only been thousands of miles away in London, but was Sabrina's father. And in hurting Templeton, exposing his behaviour to the world, he would be hurting Sabrina too.

She had still not answered his question, her wide gaze searching his face.

'Well? What was I shouting?'

He reached out and stroked an errant strand of wet

hair from her cheek behind her ear. His heart was thumping and he could not seem to take his eyes off her.

'Come on… You used to tell me your dreams back in the orphanage and I would try to interpret them. Do you remember?'

'I remember,' she whispered.

'You always trusted me then.'

'Yes…'

The dazzle of sunlight on the water reflected off her throat and face, as if her skin was rippling with light. He recalled her broken face, the scar tissue she'd tried so hard to hide as a child, and could almost see it again as the sun bounced off the water droplets running down her cheek.

'So tell me what I was shouting in this nightmare. Maybe I can work out what it means.'

'I…I don't remember,' Sabrina muttered.

But he dismissed that. Especially when she lowered her gaze, ostensibly simply not meeting his eyes, but in truth studying his semi-naked body.

He was gradually learning to recognise that new, hungry look in her face. He felt it too, that hunger and yearning to be closer to her, to join with her as one miraculous whole, as they had done once before. But he knew how dangerous that would be. And he wasn't quite crazy enough to go there. Not after last time.

His heart accelerated like soft, distant thunder. 'You don't remember?' he demanded. 'Somehow I don't believe you.'

His gaze focused on the quick, nervous lick of her lips, then dipped to the rise and fall of her chest. He knew her too well not to read the signs. She was trying to conceal something from him. But what?

His eyes narrowed on her face. 'What's the matter, Sabrina?' A thought struck him. 'Did I call out your name? Is that it?'

'What? No!'

Sabrina trod water, frantically trying to steer clear of the dangerous temptation of his body, hard and achingly muscular, muscles bulging in his chest and his flat abdomen visible through the water…

Yet still she kept drifting closer and closer, constantly having to back-pedal with her feet and legs, thrusting cooler currents of water between their two bodies, both of them so scantily clothed they might as well have been naked.

If only she had packed a one-piece swimsuit for this trip. But no, she'd chosen to pack this skimpy white and gold bikini, with its deep-plunge cleavage and tiny string briefs, thinking she would probably never wear it. And now his gaze kept straying unashamedly to her breasts, bobbing on top of the water in an embarrassing way.

Flustered, she sucked in a shaky breath, meaning to explain that she hadn't been able to interpret his incoherent dream shouts, and then he surprised her by moving closer. Startled, she stared up at him, deeply aware of his proximity, heat burning along all the pathways in her body until her skin was alight with it.

Idly, his fingers brushed her cheek again, then stroked down her throat towards the deep V of her cleavage, those dark, intelligent eyes watching for a response.

She began to say something, but the sunlight dazzled her. That and his broad shoulders, and the naked chest mere inches away, gleaming with water…

Desire burned through her in a hot flush and her eyes narrowed on his strong, muscular body. Her hands curled into fists as she battled the need to touch him in return. The world spun, frustration was molten inside her, and she gasped, abruptly light-headed, flailing her hands in the water as her head sank and water lapped at her lips.

'Sabrina…? What the hell?'

His face, dark and sombre, loomed over her, then his arms clamped about her frame and a few seconds later Rafael had lifted her bodily out of the water.

Dripping and helpless, she clung to his wet body, her hands slipping on his strong shoulders, feeling the muscles bulge and contract under her fingers.

He waded through shallow water to set her down on the pool steps, still waist-deep in water. 'What happened? Are you okay?'

'Sorry,' she whispered weakly. 'I…I got dizzy.'

'That's what comes of skipping breakfast before exercising,' Rafael chided her. He stepped back in the water, examining her with searching eyes. 'Or was it the heat? You never used to mind it. But I suppose you've been living in England a long time now.' He smiled, showing white teeth. 'Grown soft.'

She muttered something unflattering under her breath, and his smile broadened.

'I see you're feeling better,' he drawled.

It hadn't been the heat, of course, or her lack of breakfast. It had been her hyper-awareness of his body that had precipitated that sudden bout of weakness.

And he was even closer now.

All she could focus on was the sculpted perfection of his chest and the washboard abs that spoke of long hours in the gym. Her attention zigzagged wildly between the velvety darkness of his gaze and the muscular expanse of his biceps and pectorals, all manner of wickedly delicious thoughts wrecking her peace of mind.

Her self-control was beginning to shear away, leaving her defenceless.

'Hey, are you okay? You look flushed.'

Rafael lifted a hand to her cheek, and his touch inflamed her.

She had gone into this marriage with her eyes wide open, aware of how badly he could hurt her, and determined not to make a fool of herself again. But she couldn't keep fighting this attraction between them. It was tearing her apart, pretending not to want him…

Growling like an animal, she abandoned control and leant forward, setting her mouth hungrily against his with an impact that rocked them both.

As he staggered and shifted, steadying himself in the water, her arms rose to encircle his strong neck, her fingers running through sleek dark hair, grasping the back of his head.

'Rafael…' she moaned against his mouth, all pretence swept away by the hot, turbulent waves of desire washing through her. 'Yes!' she gasped, not answering his question so much as urging him on. 'Yes!'

It might be crazy, and it was definitely not in their

contract. But nobody would ever know her like he did, she thought feverishly, and the only thing that could make their oneness more absolute was for them to bring each other to completion.

His tongue thrust between her lips and she sucked on it fiercely. Rafael groaned and thrust deeper, plundering her mouth. His strong hands lifted her from the pool steps and rooted her body against him, so she was straddling his hips. Leaning back, she rubbed herself suggestively against his arousal and felt him stiffen further, his clinging swim-trunks doing little to disguise his excitement.

Their kiss deepened. He cupped her breast, his hand warm and possessive, then pulled down the wet fabric to expose bare flesh. One thumb strummed across her nipple, bringing it instantly erect. Her heartbeat accelerated as their damp, half-naked bodies whirled and strained together in the sunlit water.

'*Thee mou*, woman,' he muttered, turning his head to kiss an explosive path down her neck.

His words were incoherent, hard to make out.

'You're simply gorgeous, stunning… You have the face of a goddess.'

CHAPTER EIGHT

SABRINA FROZE BENEATH HIM. The soft, panting goddess of Greek myth was abruptly an icy-eyed viper, hissing defiance as she planted both hands on his chest and heaved him free of her body.

'Get off me,' she spat.

Rafael staggered, caught off-guard, splashing backwards into deeper water. He stared up at her in confusion as she left the pool.

'What the hell was that for?' He launched himself upright again, his adrenalin levels spiking at this unexpected attack. 'What's the matter? Did I hurt you?'

But she'd already grabbed her towel and was charging up the steps to the villa as though the devil were at her heels, not looking back.

'Sabrina, come back!'

Dripping wet, he was halfway up the steps in pursuit when he caught sight of Kyria Diakou, standing shocked on the veranda, staring down at him, a tray in her hands.

Embarrassed, his heart thumping, Rafael slicked back his wet hair and slowly retraced his steps to the poolside.

An edge of defiance laced his hot thoughts. He'd

broken the no-touching terms of their contract. But he clearly recalled *her* fingers wrapped in his hair, both *her* hands tugging him close, the provocative thrust of *her* tongue against his, and the hoarse 'Yes!' she'd uttered. Not once but *twice*.

With a sharp intake of breath he dived back into the refreshing depths of the pool, letting the water cool his ardour.

What had he done wrong? One minute she'd been urging him on, the next she'd shoved him aside. But perhaps he should give her some space to calm down before asking for an explanation. He didn't want to risk a full-blown row.

After a quick swim, he towelled off, got dressed again, and ate a light breakfast before heading upstairs to his wife's suite.

'Sabrina?' He knocked at her door. 'May I come in?'

Receiving no answer, he tried the handle and went in to find the lounge and bedroom empty. He checked the ensuite bathroom too, but she wasn't there.

Downstairs, he found Kyria Diakou dusting a large Grecian statue in the entrance hall. She looked flustered when he asked if she had seen Sabrina.

'Your wife has gone out, sir,' she told him in a faltering voice. 'Kyria Romano asked Nikos to drive her into town half an hour ago. A shopping trip, she said. I assumed you knew...'

It took all his willpower to nod with feigned calm, even muster a smile for her. 'Of course. I remember now.' He paused, made his tone casual. 'I'll join her in town.' Unhooking a baseball cap from the rack near the door, he settled it low over his forehead against the sun's glare. 'Thank you, Thea.'

Rafael always had a sports car brought to Villa Rosa for his visits. The blood-red Ferrari roared around the sharp bends of the coastal road and along the dusty straights, growling in the low gears as he slowed reluctantly for quiet villages, their windows shuttered against the heat of the day.

She could have caught a ferry by now. Gone back to the Greek mainland.

Unconsciously, he tightened his hands on the wheel and kicked his foot down on the accelerator. The Ferrari leaped forward with its characteristic throaty roar, spitting out a cloud of dust and grit behind him, visible in the rear-view mirror.

He'd gone too far in the pool—he acknowledged that. But Sabrina had initiated it…practically throwing herself at him.

A burning sense of injustice gripped him and his body tensed. He narrowed his eyes on the road ahead. He needed to master his desire for her. Yet every time he made an attempt, things slipped further out of his control.

He hadn't felt like this in years. Not since when, as a young boy, having finally broken out of the tiny space his father had imprisoned him in, he had cradled his dead mother's head in his lap, filled with self-loathing because he'd been too late to save her.

His therapist had taught him how to avoid triggering that memory 'wound', and what signs of trauma response to look for in himself. The nightmares he couldn't remember—like the one that had apparently woken Sabrina in the night—was one of those signs. And his permanently raised heart rate was another...his inability to calm down.

The rejection in Sabrina's eyes today had come dangerously close to reawakening the broken boy inside him—the one he'd lulled to sleep through therapy. And he still had no idea what he'd done to upset her.

But he was determined to find out.

The Ferrari growled as he was forced to slow down once again. The busy port was packed with tourist traffic as the incoming ferry discharged a long line of vehicles from its car deck. Rafael slotted the car neatly into the first parking space he found, then set off at a run for the terminal building, ignoring the stares of passers-by.

After grabbing Rafael in the pool and kissing him breathless, Sabrina had dashed back to her room, furious and shaking. She had dragged on a dress and begun angrily flinging clothes into her suitcase. She'd taken one look at him in that skimpy black swimwear and good old-fashioned lust had fogged up her brain until...

'You have the face of a goddess.'

Was that all he would ever see when he looked at her? The perfect mask her wealthy father had paid for so she could forget the horrors of her past? Would no longer have to face its legacy in the mirror every day?

How *dared* he, damn him?

The terrible scars she'd borne as a girl were long gone. Andrew Templeton's money had paid for the best plastic surgeons in the world.

'We'll fix you,' he'd assured her on the flight to England, flicking her scarred cheek. 'My ugly duckling will soon be a swan.'

Sure enough, within a year of arriving in England the face in the mirror had changed. She had become perfect and symmetrical. Everything smoothed out and tightened, every scar lifted, every blemish removed. Only her eyes had remained the same. Troubled and blue.

She still struggled to recognise the woman in the mirror at times. The one without the facial scars she'd lived with for so long as a child.

But her father had been delighted with the result.

'Every man on this planet is going to want you,' he'd said with satisfaction, walking around her, studying her from every angle. 'That's a weapon we can use. Once you're done with your education you can take some companies for a spin…try out that devastating smile in the boardroom.' He'd winked. 'Told you I'd fix you, didn't I? You're perfect now.'

And now, whenever she failed to achieve her goals, her father would express his disappointment, urging her to live up to her expensive face.

Andrew Templeton's love had always been conditional on her being 'perfect' inside and out. She had accepted that stark truth early on, fearful of losing her adoptive father as well as her birth mother by not living up to the potential he had seen in her at the orphanage.

Now she knew he had lied to her—been her true father all along. He had not picked her out of the crowd. She had been collected like a mislaid parcel from Left Luggage.

And now her husband had indicated that he too saw her in the same terms.

The face of a goddess, indeed!

Her face had been designed by her father and superimposed over the 'old' Sabrina—the one Rafael had never looked at twice in the orphanage, except as a friend.

Eventually common sense had reasserted itself, and Sabrina had stopped packing, sinking down on the bed instead. Rafael could theoretically sue her for breach of contract if she left now, and a court case would risk bringing their arrangement—and possibly her own personal history—into the public domain. She cringed at the thought.

But she had been determined to get out of the villa at least.

That shameless kiss in the pool…

After demanding a no-sex marriage, she had thrown herself at him without a shred of dignity. Talk about embarrassment!

Groaning, she had grabbed her handbag and run downstairs to find Nikos in the hallway, settling a widebrimmed hat on his head as he headed outside with a gardening trug on his arm.

'Oh!' she'd said, smiling brightly. 'I don't suppose you're free to run me into town?' Nikos had looked surprised, and she'd added hurriedly, 'My husband says he won't be free to take me out for several hours, and I'd like to do some shopping this morning—before it gets too hot.'

To her relief, Nikos had agreed to drive her to the

port, accepting without question her guilty lie that Rafael would be joining her later, so he need not wait for her. He had seemed uncertain about leaving her alone without any security, but she had laughed, insisting she was perfectly safe here in her birthplace.

Now she was alone, she headed for a harbourside café with tables set outside in the shade, ordered a cooling drink and turned on her phone.

The chime of messages arriving seemed never-ending. Since news of their wedding had broken her phone had received dozens of calls and messages from friends, colleagues and associates.

But the bulk were from her father.

Rage churned inside her as she read his arrogant, abusive messages. This man, who had lied and manipulated her for years, thought he could snap his fingers and she would come to heel. Tempting though it was to continue ignoring him, Sabrina knew it would be wiser to respond and play for time. But she mustn't allow herself to be drawn into confronting him about her past. Not yet…not while she still felt so fragile.

Taking a deep breath, she called him back.

Andrew Templeton answered after only two rings. 'Sabrina, thank God. I was hoping you'd call again. Are you all right?' Without waiting for an answer, he demanded, 'Is it true? Have you really lost your mind and married that low-life playboy Romano?'

She closed her eyes, battling to stay calm. If she flipped, this call would end in disaster and her father would not rest until he had found her. And right now she needed to sort this mess out for herself—not fall back on 'Daddy's' help.

'It was the only way to save the orphanage,' she said.

'Nonsense. We could have found some other leverage… These people always have a price.'

'I know,' she ground out, struggling against bitterness. 'And Rafael's price was me. But only for a year. Then we can go our separate ways. We've signed a contract.'

Her father was silent for a moment, then he said heavily, 'Very well. Give me your location. I'll send someone to bring you back home. We can get the lawyers involved and sort all this out once you're safely back on English soil.'

'I'm a big girl, Dad. I don't need to be rescued. Not this time.'

In her mind's eye she saw again Andrew Templeton's smiling face as he led her out of the orphanage, promising she would never be alone again. Naively, she had thought him the best man in the world.

'I didn't ring you for help or advice,' she added, almost choking.

It was harder than she'd expected not to admit what she knew and demand an explanation for his horrific behaviour. But her self-control was in tatters as it was. If she started down that particular path she would probably explode.

'I rang because I…I didn't want you to worry.'

'Without any friends or family present—only the paparazzi—you marry a man with Romano's criminal background…a man who treated you abominably in Paris…and you say I mustn't worry?' His voice was shaking. 'Sabrina, tell me where you are. Are you really in the Caribbean, or was that just a ruse to throw me off the scent? Because I swear, I'll soon find you.'

'Can't you just give me some space?' she pleaded.

He ignored her. 'I need to speak to you in person, and without Romano in the room. Is that clear? If you won't fly home, I'll come to you.'

'No, Dad, you mustn't try to find me,' she told him more firmly, determined not to cave to his demands. 'You need to let this go. I'll speak to you again after the honeymoon. Okay?'

Ending the call on his noisy protests, Sabrina closed her eyes, trying to calm her frazzled nerves. Slowly, she finished her drink, and then walked along the sunlit harbourside to watch the ferry reversing into its berth, lost in her own scattered thoughts and fears.

When a shout rang out along the harbour she turned at her name and found herself face to face with Rafael, her father's scathing disapproval still echoing in her ears.

'Hello, Sabrina. Going somewhere?' her husband asked tightly, jerking his head towards the ferry.

Sabrina dug her fingernails into her palms, her cheeks flaring with heat. 'It's true, I did consider catching a ferry and disappearing,' she admitted. 'But I've never given up on a business deal in my life and I won't start now.'

'So why run out on me?' he growled.

'Because you hurt my feelings and—'

'*Hurt your feelings?*' he repeated, incredulous. 'How?'

'Will you let me finish? If you don't, I'm catching the next ferry out of here.' She thrust her chin in the air at his frustrated look. 'I've just been speaking to my father. I can do without another lecture from an overbearing male who thinks he owns me, thank you very much.'

He sank his hands in his trouser pockets and glared at her from under long dark lashes. She thought at first he would refuse. But then his lips thinned.

'Very well.' His brows lifted when she still hesitated. 'Go on. Tell me about your...*feelings*, then.'

Seconds later he was following her along the quayside as she spun on her heel and marched away, too angry even to speak to him.

'*Thee mou*, would you stop a minute?' When she turned, her eyes spitting fury, he said with a sigh, 'All right. That was a patronising thing to say. I apologise.'

Sabrina was surprised, even shocked by this unexpected admission. But she still said nothing, folding her arms defensively.

'Maybe you don't see our marriage as anything but a sham,' Rafael continued, a muscle jerking in his jaw, 'but I know you haven't forgotten our past. We were good friends once, and that's not a bad foundation for a marriage. Even a one-year arrangement like ours.'

His dark gaze grew velvety dark, hypnotising her again.

'Look, I don't want to start playing the blame game here, but in the pool, you kissed *me*—not the other way around. You *wanted* me. I felt it. Then you pushed me away like I'd tried to assault you.'

His last words crackled on the air, like static in her soul.

'Care to explain?' he asked.

Their eyes clashed as guilt and confusion warred inside her. He wasn't wrong. She *had* been to blame for what had happened earlier. Yet how to explain without baring her soul and risking the kind of rejection that would probably finish her?

There were people all around them on the busy quayside, glancing curiously their way. Alone, she might not have attracted much attention. But the two of them together—Sabrina and Rafael Romano, newlyweds—would make quite a photographic coup. And then her father would know for sure where they were honeymooning...

'Let's walk, shall we?' she suggested.

He said nothing, but followed as she stalked away, head high. They crossed the road between slow-moving cars, soon heading deep into the honeycomb of narrow streets and alleyways beyond the tourist traps. The whitewashed walls of traditional Calistan homes rose on either side of the narrow lanes, their windows shuttered against the heat of the day, flat roofs bathed in sunlight and draped with washing.

He must have brought his mobile with him, because she heard it ring. He drew it out of his pocket, hesitating before glancing at her.

'Go ahead,' she said lightly, continuing to walk. 'You might as well take advantage of having a signal here.'

Rafael stopped to answer the call, catching up with her a few minutes later, an energetic look in his face. 'Looks like that big deal I've been hoping for may be going ahead. Still early days, but the mood music has definitely changed. Thanks to you,' he added softly, 'it seems I'm no longer such a bitter pill for their conservative stakeholders to swallow.'

'I'm glad to hear it.'

He studied her face, then dropped the subject. They walked on together through the quiet maze of streets.

'So, are you ready to talk yet?' He sounded brusque, almost impatient.

'Please…this is difficult for me.' Sabrina wrapped her arms about herself like a nervous teenager. 'It's true, I did kiss you first in the pool,' she admitted in a whisper. 'But that wasn't why I ran.' She fixed her gaze on the dusty stones at their feet. 'It's just…when we were kids, you didn't care about any of that.'

'Any of what?' He sounded baffled.

'My looks.'

He was silent for a moment. 'You're talking about your scars?' he said slowly. 'You think I'm only attracted to you because you've had plastic surgery?'

Tongue-tied, she made a rough noise of assent, gripping her sides tightly. Tears squeezed out from under her lids and she looked away through blurred vision, hating her own weakness.

'*Thee mou*, Sabbie… Are you serious?' He came to a halt, and she stopped too. 'You mean it, don't you?'

'You never kissed me when we were younger.'

'Yes, because we were *kids*,' he exploded, and then reined himself in, seeing her flinch. 'My lovely idiot… I am absolutely *not* attracted to you because you've had your face fixed. This thing between us is about chemistry, not beauty. Got it?'

'But you said…' she gulped '…I had *the face of a goddess.*'

'And so you do. But that's not why I find you attractive. I've dated one or two of the world's most beautiful women, remember? They had nothing on you for sheer sex appeal—trust me.'

Heartened by this flattery, she peeped up at him through wet lashes. 'Only one or two?'

'Claws in, pussycat,' he drawled.

Their eyes met and everything inside her was drawn inexorably towards him, as though he'd bound a cord about her heart and was tugging on it. She drew a long breath and felt the tension begin to drain from her body. It was difficult to ignore their long bond of friendship, and just now, when she was feeling particularly lost and lonely over her father's betrayal, perhaps it would be stupid to try.

'Very well,' she agreed reluctantly, reaching for a tissue from her bag and drying her eyes. 'Maybe I overreacted. My head's just so messed up at the moment. My father—'

'He really did a number on you, didn't he?' he said huskily.

'You don't understand. I always thought he'd arranged for plastic surgery to help me fit in better at that posh school… But he did it because he couldn't b-bear looking at my scars.'

'Sabrina, no.'

'It's true!' she burst out. 'Andrew Templeton hates any kind of imperfection. The first time he saw me, when he turned up at the orphanage, he shuddered. He actually *shuddered*.'

She felt again the searing humiliation of that moment, made a thousand times worse now, because she knew that he'd come to meet his own daughter for the first time that day.

'What a piece of work,' Rafael muttered.

'He's never let me forget it either. Whenever I make a mistake, he somehow always finds a way to reference the surgery…as though to remind me how imperfect I am under—' She choked. 'Under the mask.'

Rafael made a rough noise, trying to take her in his arms for a hug, but she stepped back, shaking her head. The last thing she wanted was to complicate matters by letting him get close again.

'No, I'm fine…' She dried her cheeks. 'I need to deal with this in my own way. Now, I'll come back to the villa with you. But—'

'I know,' he interrupted. 'No more touching.'

'Exactly.'

And no more swimming together either, she thought grimly, recalling the temptation of his bronzed semi-naked body gleaming with water.

'Better avoid kissing me, then,' he tossed back, as though reading her mind, 'if you want me to keep my hands off you. Especially when we're both wearing next to nothing.'

'No problem.'

She had spoken lightly, flippantly, but her heart was already racing again as they walked back to the car.

The real question was, could *she* keep her hands off *him*?

* * *

On the drive back to Villa Rosa, along the winding, dusty roads as familiar to him as the landscape of his mind, Rafael found it hard to concentrate on the road ahead, constantly glancing at his wife and wishing he could read her thoughts.

Her face was averted, as if she was studying the dramatic scenery of Calista, its distant, hazy hills punctuated by stately spikes of cypress thrusting dark into an azure sky.

'Did you ring your father while you were in town?' he asked.

'Yes.' She bit her lip deeply. 'I wanted to confront him. But in the end I didn't even bring it up. I couldn't trust myself not to scream at him.'

'Do you hate him now you know the truth?'

'Yes!' she said with venom, and then groaned. 'No, how can I? He's my father. But…' Her voice tailed off.

He nodded. 'It's complicated.'

She turned towards him. 'It must have been complicated for you too, though,' she said.

His hands tightened on the steering wheel, his nerves prickling as he guessed what was coming next.

'I mean, your dad… The things he did to you, and then…' She left the rest unspoken.

'Murdering my mother?' He made an effort to slow his breathing and turn his thoughts away from that flashback in his head. His mother's body, his wailing childish grief, and his hatred for the man who had done it. '"Complicated" doesn't cover it.'

'I'm sorry.'

'No need to be.' He shrugged, trying to stay casual. 'It was before you came to the orphanage.'

'True.' She was watching him curiously. 'But you never really told me what happened.'

'Would you have done, in my position?' His hands clenched even harder on the wheel, and he set his jaw as he slowed to round the next bend. 'I wanted to forget. To put it behind me.'

'I remember the boys calling you names…but I never understood why.'

'Because they were cruel. That's all you need to know. There's no point discussing ancient history.'

To his amazement, there were tears in his eyes.

Angrily, he blinked them away. 'It hardly matters now, does it?'

'I think it still matters to you.' She touched his arm. 'Though you're right—it shouldn't do. Whatever those boys thought, you've proved yourself a thousand times over since then.'

Rafael struggled to maintain focus on his driving. The villa was within sight now, its white domed roof bathed in sunlight. His refuge from the outside world. And he had never needed it more.

'Not everyone would agree with that appraisal,' he growled.

'What do you mean?'

But he only shook his head. 'Forget it.'

'Rafael—'

'I've had a few unpleasant comments, that's all. Sideways looks in the boardroom.'

'About what?'

He bared his teeth. 'My background.'

Her eyes widened. 'Don't tell me people have judged you for being an orphan, for God's sake? For coming from an underprivileged family?' There was outrage in her voice now. 'That's appalling.'

He shrugged, not wanting to make a big thing of it. 'I don't think it's held me back. I lack a few advantages, that's all. No blue blood or old school tie network.' He frowned. 'There were a few difficult moments early on in my career. I soon learnt not to advertise my personal history—let's put it like that.'

'I see...' Sabrina was silent for a moment as they approached the high gates to the villa complex. 'I hope my father doesn't take advantage of that to make your life difficult.'

'If he does, that will be my concern, not yours.'

Rafael raised a hand to the guard in the turreted gatehouse, who nodded in recognition and opened the electric gates for him to drive through.

'I'm your wife. That makes it my concern too.' Sabrina hesitated. 'And I never said a proper thank-you.'

'Thank you?' He glanced at her, puzzled. 'What for?'

Already Kyria Diakou was at the door, waiting for them, her face wreathed in smiles. No doubt she and Nikos had been unsettled by Sabrina's trip to the port alone. The older couple had not said anything, but he had not missed the unusual warmth they had shown Sabrina, and guessed they approved of his marriage and were keen for it to work.

'For telling me about my father,' Sabrina said now. 'I still feel stupid for not having realised on my own that

Andrew Templeton was my biological parent. I mean, the physical resemblance between us is obvious now. Bone structure, colouring... I just didn't see it.' She shook her head. 'I'm such an idiot.'

'Don't say that.' He had spoken harshly, and she glanced at him, surprised. 'You're not to blame. Nobody could have guessed such a thing. You're the victim here.'

'Absolutely. Though I expect my father will find a way to frame it so I'm the one to blame.' She gathered her things as he parked the car. 'We're both victims of our fathers, aren't we?'

He turned off the engine and sat unmoving. 'I'd never thought of it like that before,' he said grudgingly. 'But I suppose we are, yes.'

'Then let's agree never to be victims again,' Sabrina suggested softly. 'How's that?'

He met her eyes and saw the vulnerability there. He wished that he could make her smile again. Really smile, the way she had done when they were kids, with all her face, as if a beam of light was shining out of her soul. Somehow, Templeton had extinguished that light when he'd taken her away from Calista.

'It's a deal,' he agreed.

CHAPTER NINE

THEY ATE THAT night in near silence, neither particularly hungry, both picking at the excellent dinner served to them by Kyria Diakou. Afterwards, once the housekeeper had cleared the table and retreated, they lingered over coffee and liqueurs while the sun set over the dusky Aegean and night fell softly across Calista.

'We could take a walk in the gardens,' he suggested at last, 'if you need to stretch your legs. I don't think you've had a chance to explore the grounds yet.'

Sabrina's gaze met his over her glass of rich raspberry liqueur. Unsmiling, she tipped the glass to her lips, the ruby liquid glinting in the candlelight. When she lowered the glass and licked her lips his eyes seized on that seductive gesture, his body restless and on fire.

'Why not?' she said lightly.

He held out a hand and to his surprise she took it. He led her around the sleeping villa until they reached the formal gardens—a square courtyard open to the sky, surrounded on all four sides by a colonnade. Flowers bloomed in ornate terracotta urns and troughs, while a dolphin fountain of his own design played into a shallow pool at the centre.

Slowly, they walked around the colonnade, their path illuminated at intervals by soft solar-powered lamps. Cicadas sang in the warm darkness, and the scent of jasmine was thick on the night air. Breathing in the sweet fragrance, Rafael felt the tension of the past few days begin to drain out of him.

He had often come out here after the villa was first renovated, finding sanctuary from his high-stress lifestyle in this place of peace.

Now he was sharing it with Sabrina.

With his wife.

He came to a halt at an opening into a wider courtyard. She looked like a water nymph in the lamplit darkness, wild and seductive, her long blonde tresses haloed with light.

He brushed a long finger under her chin, tilting her face towards him, and she did not flinch away. 'Sabbie…' His nickname for her as a girl hung in the air between them, a whisper from the past. 'Sabbie,' he repeated softly, 'I'm truly sorry about your father…the lies he told you.'

'None of that was your fault.'

'No, but now you're away from him I want you to be happy again. Carefree. Like you used to be.' He examined her face. 'Tell me how I can help with that.'

'I don't think it's possible.'

'Anything's possible.'

'Is it?'

Her smile was teasing, her gentle fragrance filling his senses.

'Well, I suppose we could…change the narrative.' Slowly, suggestively, she held his gaze. 'Rewrite the past.'

His heart was thumping violently, his body tingling. 'Could you be more explicit?'

'Must I?' she whispered, but she put a hand to his face, cupping his rough cheek. 'I guess, with everything that's happened recently, I'm just so tired of feeling hurt. I want to be held. To be loved.'

When he held his breath, hardly daring to move, her voice broke.

'Forget the contract. Make love to me tonight. Please, Rafe…'

Desire flared in him, a guzzling torch fed by the husky need in her voice, the gasoline of her touch on his stubble.

'Sabbie, are you sure?'

He didn't know why the hell he was asking that. She sounded one hundred percent sure. It was he who was unsure about letting his guard down, risking his sanity and his soul. All the same, taking her by the shoulders, he brushed his lips across hers, but tentatively, still giving her time to change her mind.

'Yes!' she gasped, quickly drawing his hand up to cup her mounded flesh through the soft sea-blue fabric of her dress. She wasn't wearing a bra. 'I need you to touch me.'

His heart accelerated.

Sabrina moaned and her head fell back, exposing her throat. Palming her unrestrained breast, he bent to kiss her throat, every nerve in his body burning with excitement as his lips met fevered skin.

It was like diving into the Aegean and feeling its warm depths close about him. After the frustration of days not being able to kiss her, to make love to her as he wished, the freedom was exhilarating. His skin prickled with lightning wherever her fingers touched, moving blindly as they explored his face…

Hungrily, he parted his lips to draw those two questing fingers inside, sucking on them fiercely until Sabrina gave a muffled sob, her eyes flying open, her turbulent blue gaze like storm-tossed waves.

He scooped her up, carrying her to the large, cushioned divan beside the fountain. There, he lay her down among the red and orange cushions and knelt beside her. His need was urgent, but he must not rush her, he knew, and forced himself to slow down, to make love…

'Agape mou,' he whispered in her ear.

Her jewelled sandals were quickly disposed of. Tantalised by the glittering silver anklet, he let his fingers play with it a moment, before sliding up her shapely calf to her knee, then slipping daringly beneath her shift dress, stroking the soft flesh of her thighs.

She moaned, the foaming blue fabric of her dress ebbing away as she drew up her knees, exposing what lay beneath. 'Rafe, I need you so badly.'

There was a flush in her cheeks, a glow that told him she was in the grip of the same fever that burnt him.

'Do…? Do you need *me*?' she added.

'Never doubt it,' he growled.

'Then show me.'

Impatiently, she sat up and dragged the flimsy dress over her head, tossing it to the ground. Beneath, she wore nothing but a pair of lacy blue panties, barely enough fabric to cover her sex. Staring at him hungrily, she knelt among the divan cushions, breasts jutting magnificently, her pale body gleaming near-nude in the darkness.

'Come here, Rafe,' she ordered him in Greek, her voice thickened by desire. She tugged at her panties. 'Don't make me wait any longer.'

Equally urgent, he helped her discard the panties, and then held her naked in his arms, stroking one breast while sucking firmly on the other, revelling in the sweet taste of her flesh. In Paris, she had been shy and inexperienced. This was a different Sabrina…a woman who knew what she wanted.

He felt a stab of jealousy, wondering who had been her lover since him, then the thought was lost in the swirl of heat between them.

His tongue worked on the aroused points of her nipples and Sabrina panted and cried out, writhing beneath him. His fingers explored the sweet flesh between her thighs, stroking softly and masterfully in the damp cleft while he continued to nuzzle her breasts.

'Rafe, please…'

Her knees parted for him, her hips arching high off the cushions as she pushed against him, each sinew of her lithe body urging him to go deeper, to bring her to completion.

Over and over he rubbed his thumb across the nub of flesh and heard her gasp. Then he bent his head there. Her hands gripped his hair, his neck, his shoulders, urg-

ing him closer, her nails digging into his back like claws.
The sharp pain excited him. He hoped she had drawn
blood…marked him as her lover.

Her cries rose to a throbbing crescendo and then she
flung out her arms, gripping the cushions of the divan
and fisting the soft material, her body jerking beneath
him. He closed his eyes, driven by an urge so primitive
he could no longer control it. At last Sabrina thrust up
against his mouth, a reedy cry on her lips, and he felt a
surge of triumph that he had brought her so much pleasure, and something else besides. A strange tenderness
that shook him to the core.

He needed her too. But they had to be careful. This
was not what they'd planned.

'Are you protected?' he asked, hesitating. 'Should I
fetch—?'

'I'm on the pill,' she whispered.

He rose above her in relief, swiftly undressing now,
kicking aside his trousers, his boxers. His desire was
urgent, a hardness that was almost painful, that could
only be assuaged in her softness.

'Sabrina…' he said huskily, bringing himself between
her splayed thighs, finding again the wet heat that had
welcomed his mouth and his fingers. 'You're mine,' he
told her, thrilled by this simple truth. He stroked and ca-
ressed her slick core in readiness. 'My wife. My woman.'
Perhaps she had taken other lovers since him. But he
knew nobody else would ever know her as intimately.
'You will always be mine. My Sabrina.'

But Sabrina shook her head.

'No.' Gazing up at him through half-closed eyes, her

skin still glowing with pleasure, she whispered, 'I don't belong to anyone, Rafe. I never will again. I'm done with belonging.'

'You're mine. My wife. My woman. You will always be mine. My Sabrina.'

Did he understand why she had to reject his words of possession? Not because she didn't want this consummation as desperately as he did, but because she was still smarting from the lies she'd been fed for years—the great deception that had stunted her childhood and her youth.

She needed to be free now, to be her own person, and Rafael would have to accept that if he wanted to be her lover.

She stilled for a beat, watching him anxiously, wondering if he would turn away. But he seemed to understand the fierceness of her response. His eyes glinted above her in the darkness, his mouth quirking, showing white teeth. Then he bent over her body like a worshipper, reverently kissing her throat and breasts as the hard ridge of his arousal pressed against her, demanding entry.

'No,' he agreed, and she caught an edge of regret in his voice. 'You're a free spirit, Sabbie. But tonight at least you're mine.'

And he slid home inside her wet flesh, with a demanding thrust that snatched her breath away and drove her body temperature several degrees hotter. She felt her cheeks flare and gasped as he began to make love to her, rising to meet his thrusts, knowing herself close to the tremulous edge.

She soared among the bright points of light above her, the stars of her childhood, of Calista, while he worked at her slick flesh, his maleness intoxicating her senses. Still deep inside her, he palmed a breast, bent his head to her taut nipple and sucked hard. The pain and pleasure were too exquisite…she could scarcely bear them. Her concentration frayed. She chewed her lip, thrashed her head from side to side, trying not to scream. And then she hissed and let go, her body shuddering into joy again.

'Yes…' His growl urged her on. His face was a mask of desire now, barely recognisable. His hands smoothed her hips down into the soft cushions as he rode her, a muscular god, driving into her again and again, his dark gaze hooked on her face. 'Sabbie,' he muttered, his pace increasing. 'My Sabbie.'

They were making love again at last. It was one of her recurring dreams and now it was true. She had imagined this reunion so many times…

Sabrina closed her eyes to his magnificent body, almost overwhelmed by his power and presence, his consummate skill as a lover. Rafael shifted with ease, a hand under each knee, raising her legs to cradle them about him.

His hips angled and he drove deeper still, working the soft hot metal at her core, remaking her. Sabrina gasped and let her head fall back, losing herself to a pleasure beyond anything she had ever known, gripping the sides of the divan, its hard edges the only thing anchoring her to reality.

Even that one glorious night with him in Paris had not been like this.

But they understood each other better now.

They connected.

They soared high and burnt together in the darkness. Her body was a river of fire.

She shivered with ecstasy, her eyes flying open at last. High above, the night sky dazzled her with its silent beauty. Black velvet studded with millions of tiny jewels, arcing over their heads.

His breathing became ragged, his thrusts erratic. 'Sabrina!' he cried out.

Beyond them, the fountain played endlessly, spilling liquid into the warm depths of the pool. They lay together on the divan for some time afterwards, bare limbs tangled, facing each other, while their hearts stopped thumping and their breathing returned to normal.

Sabrina's body ached and throbbed. Everything felt different, newly awoken, as though she had just learnt some fantastical truth about herself and the world.

She wanted to share her newfound joy with Rafael, with the rebellious boy she had once known as well as she knew herself. But what if he didn't understand? What if he was no longer the boy she remembered and he laughed at her moment of revelation? What if he turned away as he had done in Paris and left her wounded and dying inside?

So she lay there and said nothing, the joy slowly cooling in her heart, a tiny precious jewel she would need to hide from everyone—even from him.

'Did you have any special plans for today?'

At the sound of his wife's voice Rafael put down his coffee cup and glanced over his shoulder. He had left Sabrina sleeping when he'd come down for breakfast, her face flushed, blonde hair spread loosely on the pillow after another late night. Studying her, he had found his mind drifting ahead to the dim and distant future, when she would leave him and demand the divorce built into their marriage contract.

He had thrust the unsettling thought far away.

It shouldn't be as hard as he feared to let her go. This phase would pass and he would be free.

What was done was done.

They were now spending every night together.

Without a word, Sabrina had moved her clothes into his suite a few days ago, and after dinner and a moonlit walk each night they retired to bed and made love as passionately and intensely as though each time might be their last. They slept deeply between bouts of lovemaking, the bedsheets hot and crumpled, their naked limbs thrown over each other in exhausted abandon...

'Not particularly,' he said now. He watched as Kyria Diakou poured fresh coffee for them both before bustling away to fetch a jug of orange juice. 'Why?'

'I'd like to go and visit the orphanage.' Sabrina sipped her coffee, her thoughtful gaze on the cloudless blue skies above the Aegean.

He couldn't seem to take his eyes off her.

It was a hot summer's day, like all the days at Villa Rosa so far. A green lizard clung motionless, partway across the warm stone wall of the veranda, watching them. Sabrina sat back in a tight red dress with a plunge neckline, crossing smooth, honey-tanned legs, and Rafael's gaze was riveted to the sexy gesture, his shorts suddenly straining. The lizard must have caught the movement too, for the creature darted away and out of sight in a flash.

As what she'd said filtered through to his brain Rafael couldn't hide his surprise. 'Again? But—'

'The new orphanage. The one in town.' She put down her cup and selected a fresh-baked sweet roll from the wicker basket. 'I want to meet the children—if that's allowed?'

'Of course. The director said I could drop in any time.'

'Good. It's important to me to know how they feel about their new home.'

She smiled at him, biting into the roll with neat white teeth. As she ate, she played with the silver chain about her neck, its diamond pendant dangling between her breasts.

'How about this afternoon? We could have lunch in town first. At that discreet little restaurant in the square.'

'Whatever you like.'

His hand crumpled the napkin beside his plate as his gaze moved hotly over her cleavage and down to the sharp inward curve of her waist.

He was falling apart already. No need to wait until she'd left him.

His control blurred.

'Sabbie…'

He was on his feet, he realised, standing right in front of her. She looked up at him, startled, eyes wide.

'You have…crumbs.' He was still gripping the napkin in his fist. 'Allow me.'

Slowly, delicately, he dabbed at the cleavage of her red dress, where two or three crumbs dusted the scarlet fabric. Sabrina watched, perfectly still except for her tongue, which crept out to moisten her lips. He shifted his gaze to her mouth at once, dropping the napkin as he leant forward to claim her lips.

She gasped and her lips parted further, their kiss deepening. He was breathing heavily, his arousal urgent now.

A sound brought him around to find Kyria Diakou in the doorway, a jug of orange juice in her hands, looking embarrassed. 'Excuse me,' she murmured, and backed away. 'I'll come back later.'

Damn it.

'No, it's fine.' He pulled Sabrina to her feet, holding her close when she would have wriggled free. 'I believe we've both finished breakfast.' He paused. 'There's no need to clear the table until later. In fact, why don't you and Nikos take the day off?'

'Sir…?' His housekeeper looked amazed.

'We'll fend for ourselves today.' When she began to stammer a protest, he shook his head. 'No, I insist.'

Once Kyria Diakou had gone, he turned to Sabrina, still clasped against him. 'How about a swim?'

'Okay, but I'll need to fetch my swimsuit.'

Rafael shook his head.

Her eyes grew large. 'Swim in the…the nude?'

'Why not?'

Her mouth opened, but then slowly closed again. A sultry look came into her face. 'You're incorrigible.'

'Maybe,' he agreed in a murmur. 'But you,' he continued, lifting her wrist to his mouth and kissing the delicate skin there, her feminine fragrance driving him wild, 'are my drug of choice. And I'm addicted.' He nuzzled her palm. 'I need to take you. And take you. And take you again.'

She swayed against him, a flush in her cheeks. 'Rafe…'

He scooped her up in his arms and carried her down the broad steps to the pool, setting her lightly on her feet by the shallow end. Holding her gaze, he drew her scarlet dress up over hips and breasts in one smooth movement, then past her head. Beneath, she was wearing matching bra and panties in flimsy red lace.

Hungrily, Rafael admired her stunning figure, then reached around to unsnap her bra, his gaze intent on the high bounce of her breasts as they were released. Then he hooked his thumbs in the waistband of her red panties and smiled as she helped him remove them too, lifting her ankles and kicking them impatiently aside.

Far from being shy in her nudity, Sabrina stood on tiptoe and set her mouth to his. He held her close, his hands sliding down to rest on her hips. Her tongue played against his, teasing and playful, and his groin throbbed with need.

'Now you,' she whispered against his mouth.

He grasped his T-shirt to drag it off, but she got there first, shaking her head.

'That's my job,' she told him, her eyes dancing.

Obediently, even though he was chafing to be free to do as he wished with her delectable body, he stood with his arms by his sides as she undressed him too, pulling off his T-shirt, then unzipping his shorts and drawing them off with painstaking care.

Rafael was breathing harshly by the time she bent with a smile to remove his distended trunks. He groaned at the maddening brush of her hands, arching his hips to meet her touch.

'Have pity, Sabrina,' he told her, his voice strangled.

She turned to descend into the shallows of the pool and his gaze followed her. There was a series of steps under the water, and she took these swiftly, sinking into the pool up to her waist before swimming away, her golden hair floating wide like a mermaid's.

He dived after her, pursuing her underwater for a few metres before surfacing close to the wall, his hands already on her waist, pulling her against his naked body. She turned to face him, her pale gleaming breasts pushing at his chest, their legs tangling...

'I need you,' he whispered against her damp throat. 'Now.'

'But what if the Diakous see us?'

'I told them to go home... If they're still here, too bad.'

Her wet lashes rose and fell and her gaze met his, those blue depths somehow strong and vulnerable at the same time.

Do it, she mouthed, almost daring him.

In one swift move he raised her effortlessly, shifting her full weight onto his hips, and draped her thighs around him. Their mouths met and his heart hammered, everything inside him straining towards her. His fingers found her core, the slippery flesh hot and yielding, more than ready for him. He worked at the delicate bud there, firm but gentle, sensing her climax as it built.

Once she'd moaned against his mouth he couldn't wait any longer. He speared inside her and felt Sabrina jerk at his entry, her cry one of satisfaction as she undulated against him.

At first he thought he had himself well under control. But then she leant back in the water, her firm thighs gripping him, and he drove deep, again and again, finally releasing himself into her with a hoarse shout. The pleasure that filled him at that moment was so intense, so overwhelming, he felt again the piercing sweetness he'd known in Paris…

Only he didn't weep this time. He closed his eyes against the water's dazzling brilliance and counted silently to ten as his heart rate returned to normal. This was a coping mechanism he used in other stressful situations, and Rafael wasn't sure why he'd chosen to do it now. Except that it allowed him to retain control.

He could barely stand afterwards, and yet somehow he managed to restore her to the shallow end, staggering towards the steps with her in his arms.

'I don't have a towel,' she protested as he set her on her feet beside the pool.

'So?' He flashed her an irreverent grin. 'Why not drip-dry?'

He waited, expecting some glib remark in response, but she stretched out on a lounger, saying nothing.

Rafael slicked back his wet hair, studying her averted profile in surprise. They were still friends, but friends with benefits now. And the sex was incredible. Sabrina was fantastically responsive as a lover, and the way she had ridden him in the pool just now, with zero inhibitions, had blown his mind.

Yet there was a barrier between them that had not existed when they'd made love in Paris, and although there was no earthly reason why that should bother him, it did.

He turned away, saying lightly, 'I'm going for a shower,' and headed up the steps into the villa without waiting for a response.

This was only a temporary marriage of convenience, he reminded himself. They might be sleeping together now, but if Sabrina could play it casual, so could he.

Later that afternoon they traversed the dusty backstreets of the Calistan port together, coming out into a new-build area, pleasantly shaded, with a high-rise complex bordered by well-maintained gardens behind security fencing. She could smell cooking, and heard loud, cheerful music playing from inside.

Above the entrance doors was a sign in Greek that read, *Calista Children's Sunshine Centre*, with a smiley icon beside it in yellow and orange.

A dark-haired girl was peering out through one of the upper windows as they were buzzed through the security gate. Something about her wide-eyed stare reminded Sabrina of her own childhood in the old orphanage. She had thought herself all alone after her mother's death, adrift in a dark world. Yet her father had been aware of her existence the whole time and had left her to languish there for years.

She thrust the angry thought away, still smarting from her father's betrayal.

'This used to be the old market,' Rafael told her as she stared about, taking in the bright, ultra-modern setting. 'When the orphanage came up for sale I had this site redeveloped and kitted out to accommodate the orphans.' He gestured up the steps to the entrance. 'Shall we?'

Sabrina smiled, but inwardly she was feeling shaky. The more they made love, the more distant Rafael was becoming. She didn't understand it, but wondered if it might be her fault. For she was aware of a growing coolness between them now that they were lovers. The marriage that had worked as a business arrangement seemed doomed to fall apart now that they were sharing a bed...

The new director, Anka, was a friendly Polish-born woman in her thirties, who seemed delighted to see Rafael and insisted on showing them around the whole orphanage herself. Her Greek was excellent. She told them several of the new children were from Poland and neighbouring Ukraine, which had inspired her to apply for the job.

Room after room was bright and sunny, with colourfully painted walls and soft matting underfoot. The kids had a large, well-equipped computer room, a television lounge with beanbags and huge sofas, a recreation area with a climbing wall and table tennis, and bedrooms with only one or two beds each, prettily decorated with ensuite bathroom facilities. Through the tinted windows, Sabrina looked down on shaded lawns and flowerbeds, and an enclosed playground for the younger children, plus a half-pipe and skater park for the older kids, all painted in bright graffiti style.

'This is marvellous,' Sabrina admitted. 'When I think of how you and I grew up... Not that the wardens didn't take care of us. But this is another world.'

Rafael nodded sombrely, his dark eyes intent on her face.

Anka gave them both a broad smile. 'And now, Kyria Romano, perhaps you would like to meet some of the children?'

'Oh!' Sabrina put her hands to her cheeks. 'Could we?'

'Of course. I've asked my assistant to gather the older children together in here.'

The director led them into the lounge area.

Sabrina recalled herself as a teenager: wary, inquisitive, permanently poised to reject the world while simultaneously eager to engage with it. These youngsters were no different. Some scrambled to their feet, staring wide-eyed at the newcomers. Others turned their backs, arms folded, eyes downcast, determined not to show any interest. One boy—with spiky hair and a black T-shirt with a superhero on it—swore loudly, and the girl beside him, who had just dropped his hand, giggled nervously.

The director began to reprimand the boy for swearing but Rafael shook his head, saying it didn't matter.

He strolled forward and held out a hand to the boy, who shook it after a moment's hesitation.

'I'm Rafael Romano. I don't believe we've met. I had a T-shirt like that when I was your age. Never too soon to be aspirational.' He grinned. 'What's your name?'

The boy introduced himself, adding, 'Romano? Are you the man who bought the orphanage?' When Rafael nodded, his eyes grew larger, his look more friendly. 'Thank you. This place is a…a miracle.'

'Especially the computer room,' one of the other kids burst out, coming closer.

'And the sports pitch.'

'Don't forget the skate park. That's awesome!'

A dark-haired girl who'd been reading in the corner put down her book, smiling up at him shyly. 'Thank you for the library too. So many stories… I'll never read them all.'

'This is Cora,' Anka said, beckoning the girl forward. 'She's a very clever girl, top of all her classes. Our resident bookworm too.'

She was the child at the window, who'd watched them come in through the gates, Sabrina realised, and she smiled at the girl warmly.

'I'm glad you approve, Cora,' her husband was saying. 'Though if you like books you really should speak to my wife, Kyria Romano. She loves reading too.'

Rafael turned to indicate Sabrina, who had not said much yet, almost as shy as the children.

'Back in the day, my wife was an orphan here on Calista, just like me. In fact, she's worried that some of you may miss the old orphanage.' He gave the children an encouraging smile. 'So, how about you tell Sabrina which one you prefer? This place or the old one?'

They spent some hours at the orphanage, chatting to the kids and later walking outside in the shade under fragrant pines. Sabrina got on well with young Cora, whose love of books and reading was expressed in short, ecstatic bursts followed by nervous laughter. It was obvious the young people loved their new location in the port and would rather not go back to the crumbling old orphanage.

After they'd finally said their goodbyes, Sabrina and Rafael wandered back to the car, smiling at each other shyly as they discussed what they'd seen. Meeting the children, so like themselves at the same age, seemed to have rekindled their friendship.

It was only when Rafael was driving them back to the villa that he broke the good mood.

'You're still coming to the charity ball in Paris, aren't you? You agreed to attend the event with me,' he reminded her, his eyes on the road ahead. 'To silence any remaining doubters and meet a few of my business associates.'

Her soul grew cold again at his words. For a short time she'd forgotten this wasn't a real marriage, that she was only his wife for a year and had official duties to perform…like a hired escort.

'Of course,' she said without expression, and turned to study the rugged sunlit landscape flashing by. 'I'll be there.'

CHAPTER TEN

THE ELEGANT PARISIAN ballroom had been decorated for the charity ball with gigantic urns spilling over with flowers, each urn set at intervals in front of floor-to-ceiling mirrors, above which spanned a glorious ceiling mural depicting what looked like gods and goddesses. The space was packed with wealthy, young, designer-clad couples whirling gracefully, while big ticket donors chatted in groups, champagne glasses in hand. Musicians played on a central raised platform, and the music swelled to a crescendo as Rafael led Sabrina through the crowded space towards the dancers.

Her husband looked unspeakably edible in a sharp designer suit, his black jacket hanging open to reveal a white silk shirt left unbuttoned to partway down his chest.

As they stood on the edge of the dance floor, it became increasingly obvious they had become the centre of attention. Everywhere she looked eyes studied them covertly, curious and speculative. From the eyes of those gossiping behind their hands on the sidelines to the smiling, uniformed staff circulating discreetly with trays of champagne and dainty, exquisitely crafted canapés.

'Shall we?' Rafael asked.

The dark slash of his eyebrows arched in query at her hesitation.

'What? You don't want to dance?'

He placed their empty champagne flutes on a passing waiter's tray and reached for her hand, his touch electrifying. Sabrina caught her breath, her whole body tingling with sensation.

'We're supposed to be in love, remember?' His gaze clashed with hers when she stubbornly refused to move. 'How will it look if we come to a charity ball together, but don't dance?'

'It's not that,' she whispered, not wanting anyone else to hear. 'It's just…everyone's staring.'

'Of course they're staring.' His voice dipped. 'Isn't that why we're here? To be seen out in public as a couple?' His fingers curled about hers, strong and possessive. 'You're a blushing new bride, remember? Try to act the part.'

She gave an automatic smile, but behind it she felt slightly sick.

'Try to act the part.'

Had Rafael been acting a part since their wedding? Making love to her so passionately, sharing his days and nights with her, just to keep her from growing restless? The boy she had known had grown into a ruthless billionaire, after all, just like her father. She wouldn't put it past him to lull her into acquiescence with such tactics.

Her phone buzzed in her sparkly clutch bag, but she

ignored it. It was probably another message from Andrew Templeton, in response to the text she'd sent him last night.

I know the truth about you, Dad. I never thought you could disappoint me. But I was wrong. Now I need time to think. Please leave me alone.

On Calista it had all felt too raw, too visceral for her to handle—remembering her childhood as an orphan, the appalling loneliness she'd experienced that first year after losing her mother, the sense of having nobody to turn to… Nobody except Rafael, that was.

But being in Paris again, where she had first escaped Andrew Templeton's suffocating control, had switched on a light inside her—a beam of courage to illuminate a new path. It had taken her a long time to get the wording of her message right. But the time had finally come to confront her father, and she was determined to do it on her terms—not his.

After hitting 'Send' and turning off her phone, she had fallen into the soundest sleep she'd enjoyed in years, waking refreshed and with an odd feeling of liberation… like a caged bird whose prison door had been left open.

They had taken an elite suite at the Paris Ritz, with two opulent bedrooms and a huge gold and white sitting room with a fabulous view of Place Vendôme and the city beyond. It had not taken long for word to get around, and the paparazzi had come swarming into the hotel lobby in search of a candid shot of the world's most famous new couple.

They had deliberately allowed themselves to be snapped, even stopping sometimes to pose for the press, hand in hand as they were now, smiling at each other. Keeping up the appearance of happy newlyweds for the sake of his business contacts.

On Calista they had made love as though the world were ending, and yet... She had never quite been sure what he was thinking or feeling. Or indeed if he was feeling anything at all. Given the absence at the heart of both their childhoods, she had often thought they should be more open to the idea of love. Yet Rafael seemed to view emotion with such disdain and suspicion, his difficult past no doubt colouring his responses.

Now they were in Paris, with its wide boulevards and elegant monuments...its intimate little restaurants and breathtaking views.

The city of love.

The irony was not lost on her.

Since their arrival in Paris, Rafael had spent every morning working, catching up with his PA in New York, while Sabrina had taken work-related calls from her own assistant, Shelley, in London. The afternoons had been spent together, exploring the famous European city and ignoring the curious looks of passers-by who recognised them.

They had taken a *bateau mouche* along the River Seine, toured the Louvre with guidebooks in hand, and strolled around the lively Rive Gauche area in the sunshine before heading to a lively club for dinner and dancing in Montmartre. Rafael was an interesting companion, keen on art, opinionated about politics without becoming dogmatic, and always able to make her laugh with a barbed remark or a clever play on words.

Paris was working its magic on them all over again. She had felt quite different in his company since arriving here, enjoying the two of them being out in the world together, openly a couple.

She was in danger of feeling something for this man that she couldn't risk admitting. Their lovemaking had lulled her into forgetting that this was a business partnership, nothing more. It would break her apart to trust him as she had trusted the younger Rafael…to open her heart only for him to walk away and abandon her exactly as he'd done before. As everyone else in her life had done, in fact.

Besides, she'd spent too many years in her father's shadow. She refused to escape from Andrew Templeton only to bind herself to yet another charismatic male— to become Rafael's lover and helpmate instead of an independent woman, walking her own path, making her own decisions.

The band had struck up a new tune with a sweeping rhythmic beat. A waltz.

They had danced a waltz last time, giggling as Rafael fumbled the steps, never having been taught ballroom dancing—unlike her.

Sabrina breathed hard through another cresting wave of anxiety, as traumatic memories jostled for space in her head. She had been so sure she could handle being in Paris with him again. Yet this was the same ballroom where they'd bumped into each other five years ago and ended up in bed…with such disastrous consequences for her heart.

Talk about *déjà-vu*.

Rafael tugged her hand, pulling her onto the dance floor. 'Come on, let's show them how to do it.'

Her eyes widened. 'But this is a waltz,' she reminded him in an urgent whisper. 'You know you can't waltz.'

He tucked his raised hand into hers, his gaze arrowing in on her face. 'After last time I made sure to take formal dance lessons. Like for horse-riding.' The dark gaze intensified, almost setting her alight, and his lip curled. 'Couldn't have the street urchin from Calista embarrassing himself in front of his betters again, could we?'

He swung her out among the other dancers, one arm anchored firmly about her waist, and suddenly they were waltzing. It felt more like flying…

'Oh!' She swallowed, looking him in the eye.

His hand clasped hers. Their bodies were intimately close. His muscular thighs brushed her body quite deliberately. The delicate silk of her blue evening gown was no barrier to the hard ridge of his arousal. Heat swamped her cheeks and her lips parted as she sought to control her breathing. His desire could not have been more prominent, though she took some comfort from the realisation that only the two of them knew about it.

His eyes glinted, his smile mocking her. 'Did I mention you look beautiful in that frock?'

'No,' she said faintly, 'but thank you.'

'You can thank me later,' he murmured, drawing her even closer as they swung around the edge of the dance floor, where a crowd of partygoers stood watching. His dark mocking gaze met hers. 'And stop looking so frightened.'

Her eyes flashed at him. 'I am *not* frightened. I told you. I don't like being stared at, that's all.'

'Yes, I remember that about you.' His voice dropped to a whisper that prickled her nerve-endings. 'But those days are over, Sabbie. You're not that lost little girl any more.'

'Aren't I?' Her hand trembled in his and she felt his grip tighten.

'Not even remotely,' he insisted.

She wished she could share his confidence. She had spent the morning trawling elite Parisian boutiques for tonight's ballgown, aware that this was a special performance—not merely for Rafael's more conservative business associates but for her father too. She knew he would scan any photos or footage of this evening like a detective looking for weaknesses in an alibi—it needed to be pitch-perfect.

Meanwhile, since that text she'd sent, her muted phone had become jammed with missed calls from Andrew Templeton, while the few messages he'd left had been brusque and uncompromising.

Call me. We need to talk. NOW.

So far she had ignored his demands, despite the nerves churning inside her at the thought of his growing anger, and had focused on herself instead.

Before the ball she'd been expertly made-up, her nails manicured and painted, her hair dressed to perfection, pampered and fussed over by the team of beauticians and an exclusive hairdresser who had come to their suite for added privacy. Then she had been helped into the snug-fitting blue silk gown, and added a few elegant diamonds to provide the finishing touches to her outfit.

Rafael, on the other hand, looked rough and on edge this evening, as though he'd barely slept in days. Still drop dead-gorgeous, though, and his designer stubble made her want to run her fingertips over his jutting chin.

'What are you thinking?'

His dark gaze scoured her face, a frown tugging his brows together.

When she didn't answer, he continued in a harsh voice, 'Forget the past. Forget your father. Think about the future, Sabrina.'

Her lips compressed as she took that in.

'Do you remember what you said when you left me in Paris last time?' she asked, daring to reopen that old wound. 'You said *I* was a part of your past, and all you wanted was to look ahead to the future.'

'Did I?' He glanced at her casually, and then looked away, though his arm tightened about her waist.

'If that was true,' she said, 'why come all the way from New York to see me on Calista? You could have explained about my father over the phone…or sent someone else to do it.'

He didn't answer for a moment, then growled, 'You know why.'

'No, I really don't.'

'Because I care for you,' he said, his voice dangerous. His stubborn chin jutted as he looked away, checking their path through the other dancers. 'We were always there for each other as children, Sabbie, and I knew I owed it to you to break the bad news in person.'

She swallowed, emotion churning inside her at his words.

'I care for you.'

Was that as good as it was ever going to get between them?

But what did she feel for him? Did she even know?

Rafael glanced down at her, his dark gaze veiled by his lashes. 'Do you remember that summer festival on Calista, the year before Templeton took you away? You would have been fifteen… We slipped away from the orphanage that night and climbed onto the taverna roof to watch the procession go past.'

His hand gripped hers as she stared into his face, feeling the bittersweet memory burning her soul.

'Afterwards, there was dancing in the street until gone midnight.'

'I remember,' she said huskily.

'You said something to me that night,' he went on, his face stony, as unmoving as an ancient Greek statue. 'Something I've never forgotten.'

Heat bloomed in her cheeks as she realised what he meant. Lying on the taverna roof and watching the women in tight, colourful dresses below, gyrating with their partners in the street, she had whispered to him, 'The first time I dance like that, I want it to be with you, Rafe.'

Rafael had looked embarrassed at the time, and she'd

regretted saying it. They had been friends, and that was all. Now, though, his eyes glowed as he met hers.

'When we met again here in Paris, what you'd said was in my head when I asked you to dance. Only I messed things up, didn't I?'

His hand tightened on hers and she knew he didn't mean the dance steps.

'For what it's worth,' he went on, his voice grating low in her ear, 'I'm sorry. I hurt you and that was un-forgivable.'

He still hadn't explained why he'd left her so abruptly in Paris the morning after making love to her for the first time. But he had at least apologised for the hurt he'd caused her, and without being prompted to do so.

She hugged that sustaining thought to herself as they whirled about the floor for the last few sweeping beats of the dance, the two of them clamped together in a heated physical awareness of each other.

After the waltz came more champagne and canapés while they worked the room together, meeting other guests and celebrity ticket-holders. She struggled against the urge to drag him away to some private room where they could talk properly. This event was about him and his business. Not their marriage.

As the glittering evening wore on, Rafael introduced her to some high-profile business associates of his that he'd recognised across the ballroom, including one of the world's wealthiest men, and she smiled and chatted by his side about their wedding and their honeymoon, playing her part with ease.

He wanted a trophy wife? He could have a trophy wife.

But inside she longed for more—for this marriage to be real—all the while knowing it could never be. She didn't attract people; she repulsed them. Everyone she had ever loved had abandoned her. Why should this time be any different?

'Thank you,' Rafael murmured afterwards, steering her away from one of the conservative Americans he was eager to do business with. 'I appreciate you keeping your side of the bargain.'

She said nothing, but her heart plummeted. It was stupid to feel hurt by his reminder of their contract. This was why they had come to Paris, wasn't it? And yet she did feel hurt.

Towards midnight, the party began to break up, the guests slowly drifting out of the grand Parisian ballroom towards the cloakrooms and the exit.

Sabrina, flagging with fatigue by then, was shocked to find herself face to face with an unexpected array of journalists and television cameras in the vast lobby. As she and Rafael descended the stairs together, arm in arm, the cameras began to flash wildly, dazzling and intimidating her. Suddenly traumatised afresh, still struggling to come to terms with her unfamiliar identity as Mrs Romano, she knew she couldn't stomach yet more questions from the paparazzi.

She trembled, looking around blindly. 'Quick, let's find another way out.'

But Rafael bent to her ear. 'No, this is why we came here. To be seen by the paparazzi.'

His intense gaze collided with hers—a jolt that ran through her like lightning.

'I never figured you for a coward, Sabrina.'

Dazed, and slightly the worse for champagne, she stumbled on the stairs in her high heels. Rafael caught her at once and pulled her close. Her hands pressed against his chest and their gazes meshed. Cameras flashed and a cry went up from the watching press. Wildly, she acknowledged bone, muscle, sinew…the heat of his body.

And the fact that he was right, of course.

This was why they had come to Paris, after all. To be publicly acknowledged as newlyweds. If she refused to speak to them now, the paps might run a story about how she was a reluctant bride, fuelling her father's paranoia about Rafael and casting doubt on their 'happiness'. Then their pretence tonight would have been for nothing.

'All right, I'll do it,' she whispered, and he led her forward to face the cameras and the shouting paparazzi, his arm about her waist.

'Miss Templeton!' came the shout. 'This way, Sabrina! Smile!'

More flash photography…and the overwhelming sense of being a creature under a microscope.

She drew herself up in front of the press, thankful at last for her training at the exclusive finishing school she'd hated. Her mouth even found a smile.

'I'm not Miss Templeton any more. Do I need to introduce my husband? Of course not—you all know him already. Rafael Romano…now a respectable married man.'

There was general laughter from the journalists.

'Is it true you've been forced into this marriage against your will, Sabrina?' one of the reporters shouted.

Rafael swore under his breath, then demanded in astonishment, 'Who the hell has been saying that?' as though he had no idea.

'Andrew Templeton,' the reporter replied. 'Your wife's father.'

They were all looking at her expectantly.

'I can't imagine why my father would say such a thing,' she told them, furious at Andrew Templeton's interference. 'I...I don't know what you've been told, but I certainly wasn't coerced into this marriage.'

It was tempting to expose her absent father for the liar and fraud that he was. But this was neither the time nor the place for such a revelation. Besides, that was not the kind of publicity they had sought in coming here.

'Rafael and I have known each other since we were children,' she continued, her voice wobbling a little. 'We grew up together on a beautiful Greek island called Calista. Both of us were orphans, with no one to turn to. My father clearly disapproves of our marriage, and that makes me sad. But I assure you that Rafael and I are very much in love.'

His fingers curled about hers, drawing her inexorably closer to his side. Their hips bumped and her body flushed with heat. Her cheeks were on fire as she glanced up at his dark, forbidding face—a look that triggered another barrage of blinding camera flashes as the photographers scrabbled to capture the perfect shot of them together.

'I'm only sorry we couldn't invite more press to c-cover our wedding,' she stammered. 'But privacy is important to us. It's no fun getting married in a goldfish bowl.'

'What do you say to your father's accusation, then?' someone shouted from the back, and everyone looked at her expectantly. 'He claims Rafael's keeping you prisoner.'

Sabrina stared at the reporter, shocked. How much lower was her father prepared to go to keep control of the narrative?

'My…my father…' she began, sorely tempted to expose Andrew Templeton's true nature in front of the world's press.

And then she swallowed what felt like a throatful of broken glass, her vision blurred with tears. This was neither the time nor the place to accuse her father of wrongdoing. She had not even spoken to him in person yet. Yet these intrusive questions had her on the verge of weeping…unable to go on. A tearful, incoherent answer would make them think she really was a prisoner, when the only thing keeping her prisoner was her heart.

Rafael knew any rebuttal of that accusation must come from Sabrina or nobody would believe it. But he'd been gritting his teeth against the urge to protect her from these vultures, and when her voice had faltered one glance at her face had sent his blood pressure soaring.

Sabrina Templeton had matured into a confident businesswoman, sharp-witted and able to handle even the trickiest of negotiations. Yet he saw the vulnerability others missed, tucked away behind the smooth mask of perfection one of the world's finest plastic surgeons had created for her.

They had history together. To him, she would always

be Sabbie, the scarred little girl who'd played with him in the dusty sunlit yard of the orphanage, and he missed the uncomplicated companionship of those days.

Her beauty was ethereal tonight. Her golden hair was worn up in a chignon, leaving her slender pale neck on display, adorned with a diamond necklace. She looked like a princess from a story book, he thought. A swan princess.

He recalled her sitting with young Cora in the library at the new orphanage, their heads bent together over a book, and an idea came to him.

Rafael smiled down at her encouragingly. 'I think we should tell them about our big plan, darling,' he said, raising his voice above the shouts of the paparazzi.

'Plan?' she repeated, blinking.

The reporters instantly forgot their previous question and went crazy, calling out, 'What's your big plan, Sabrina? Tell us!'

'Erm…' Sabrina drew a shaky breath, the fine silk sheen of her ballgown catching the light as her chest heaved. 'Why don't *you* tell them about it, Rafe?' she said. Her eyes sought his, their blue perfectly matched to her gown, a sea of churning intensity. 'Since it was your idea in the first place?'

Those eyes…

He had nearly drowned in them five years ago in this very building, reunited with her at the charity ball. He had felt the wildest leap of joy on seeing her across the ballroom, and then to his delight had seen an answering joy in her face as they'd rushed together and embraced.

The years had fallen away, and with them the hurt of her long silence.

Seduced by her light, bubbling conversation, her infectious laughter and those shy, darting looks that had told him she wanted him as much as he wanted her, they had gone back to her hotel room and made love.

Their earlier friendship had been replaced by adult passion. Touching and kissing her that night had been as natural as breathing. And when she'd whispered in his ear, 'I'm on the pill,' he had wrongly assumed an experience she hadn't possessed.

Because she'd been a virgin. Her wide eyes and muffled cry as he'd entered her had told him as much, though he had said nothing, lost in the moment.

At first, Rafael had been thrilled by her innocence, imagining she must have been saving herself for him. He had lost control, felt tears in his eyes at the moment of climax, and had held her close for hours afterwards, all his hard certainties about life softened into an emotional blur. Then, after the most mind-blowing, exquisite night of lovemaking, he had woken in the sharp dawn light to realise he never wanted to let her go—that he was in love with her.

And he'd fled like a coward, barely able to look her in the face, after saying something unforgivable.

He had run out of fear. Fear of losing her as he'd lost his mother. Fear of not being strong enough to look after her. Fear that she must eventually realise his weakness and reject him...

He had behaved like an idiot by not admitting to his fears, allowing her to think he didn't care about her.

And then he had compounded that error on Calista by convincing himself that she was merely a temporary solution to a business issue, afraid to look too deeply at his motives.

But he had not lost her yet. There was still time to make amends, wasn't there?

'As you wish, *agape mou*,' Rafael told her now. Smiling, he wove his fingers with hers, holding up their joined hands to the press pool. 'My wife and I plan to launch an international charity,' he announced, improvising swiftly. 'Our goal is to support and protect orphans all over the world.'

Shouts rang out from the assembled paparazzi, but he shook his head.

'I don't have all the details for you yet. But we'll be putting together a proposal soon. Orphans are very special and vulnerable members of any community, and not enough is being done on a global scale to help them—not only when they are children, and deserving of both loving care and secure, comfortable housing, but as young people in need of training and opportunities that might have been out of reach to them in the past.'

He saw surprise in Sabrina's eyes, and softening delight too, and raised her hand to his lips.

'Now, if you'll excuse us, my wife and I are still on our honeymoon—and, as the lady said, we'd appreciate some privacy.'

The paparazzi laughed and shouted more questions as the cameras flashed around them. But Rafael was already guiding Sabrina out to the limousine waiting for them by the kerb. They slid inside and the door closed, shutting out the chaos and the jagged, pulsing lights of the city.

'A charity for orphans… That's such a lovely idea,' she said huskily as the long, sleek car pulled away into the Parisian traffic, engine purring. 'Were you serious about it?'

He nodded. 'It's something I've been toying with for years.'

'Me too.'

'Then we'll do it,' he said firmly. 'Whatever else happens, at least we'll have built this charity together.'

CHAPTER ELEVEN

BACK IN HER bedroom at Villa Rosa, Sabrina woke with a start, sitting bolt-upright in bed. The sheet had fallen away, and her bare skin was icy-cold from the air conditioning.

She blinked at the darkness, confused.

Something had woken her.

According to the luminous digital clock beside her bed it was gone three o'clock in the morning. Roughly four hours since she and Rafael had returned to the villa. They had said a muted goodnight to each other before heading wearily for their own bedrooms, tired after their flight from Paris to Athens, followed by a turbulent helicopter ride back to Calista.

'Whatever else happens, at least we'll have built this charity together.'

His words echoed through her, slicing into her heart.

'Whatever else happens...'

Rafael was already bored and looking ahead to the end of their year together...to the no-contest divorce built into their contract. What else could he have meant?

She stumbled out of bed, dragging on a silk robe,

and slid open the balcony window, listening to the lap of the Aegean against the rocks below in the warm, velvety darkness.

A hoarse cry split the silence, jolting her heart with fright, and she realised that was what had woken her earlier. Rafael was having another nightmare.

Sabrina hurried onto the landing, flicking on the light. 'Rafael?'

She caught a shout from inside his suite, and then a series of sobs, torn with anguish as if from a tortured soul, followed by the sound of gasping.

Tiptoeing along the landing, she tried the door to Rafael's suite. It opened onto darkness. She crept tentatively inside, groping her way along the wall and into the master bedroom. The light that trickled through the open door showed her the bronze of a hunched shoulder in his vast bed, a dark head lost amid a jumble of white pillows.

As usual, he was sleeping in the nude, only a sheet covering his lower half. The crumpled silk left little to the imagination, contouring his maleness and outlining strong, muscular thighs.

As she began to back away Rafael shuddered and gave another low cry, muttering in Greek, and she realised that he was still in the grip of the nightmare. He rolled over in a fast, convulsive movement, the sheet falling away to expose taut buttocks.

Clapping a hand to her mouth, Sabrina gasped. Her blood ran hot as she struggled to control her hunger for him.

Then Rafael cried out an obscenity. She was ripped

from her dizzying need by that howl of pain, felt her face suffuse with guilt as she recalled why she had crept in here in the first place.

'Rafael, wake up…' she whispered, and hurried over to touch his shoulder. His skin was damp and hot, as though he were running a fever. Was he sick?

As she watched, he tipped onto his back again, his spine arching off the bed, feet pedalling as though running from some pursuer in his dream.

'No,' he muttered to himself. His body thrashed about, shaking the bed, and his feet tangled in the silk sheet. 'No…'

'You're having another nightmare,' she said, more loudly. 'Wake up!' When this didn't work, Sabrina reluctantly shook his shoulder. 'Rafael, you're dreaming. Can you hear me?'

To her alarm, his hand shot out, and with one smooth movement he dragged her onto the bed beside him. Before she could escape he rolled towards her, holding her close. His eyes were closed, his face flushed with sleep, and he was showing no awareness of his surroundings.

Gingerly, she attempted to slip out of his embrace and return to her room. But he seemed to sense this, his arms tightening around her in response.

He shuddered again and buried his face in her neck. 'No, please don't go… I'm sorry. I'll never do it again.'

He began to tremble violently again, abruptly releasing her.

'Wait, you can't leave me.'

Rolling over again, his back to her now, he began to claw at the sheet like a trapped animal.

'It's so hot and dark. I can't breathe. Please don't go, Papa!' His voice sounded like a frightened child's. 'Let me out of here!'

Papa.

She lay motionless beside him on the bed, listening to Rafael dreaming about his father—the man who had murdered his mother before killing himself. Only it sounded more like a memory than a dream…

Horror crept through her, turning her insides to ice.

'Rafael,' she whispered, and raised a hand to stroke his hair. 'It's Sabrina. I'm here. It's okay, you're not alone.'

He thrashed his legs again briefly, and then his breathing, which had become laboured, slowly began to return to normal.

She stayed where she was, nestled close at his back, until the heat pumping from him forced her to sit up and peel the silk robe off her body, needing to cool down. At that instant he stirred and rolled towards her. She saw the glitter of his eyes through the darkness.

'Sabrina? What are you doing here?' His voice was hoarse with surprise. He sat up, noticing the open door to his suite, the light from the landing. 'What…? What is it? Is something wrong?'

'You had another bad dream,' she admitted, but didn't embarrass him with any details. 'I heard you cry out, so I came in to see if you were okay.' Acutely aware of her own nudity, she fumbled for the silk robe to cover herself, saying, 'You're awake now, so I'll go back to bed.'

'No,' he said thickly, catching at her hand as she tried to pull on the robe. His gaze crashed against hers, hotly demanding. 'Please don't go.'

'Please don't go.'

The refrain from his nightmare.

Her pity turned to desire at the look in his eyes. She held her breath, fearing to move. Something leapt between them in the darkness—a spark that raced greedily into flame and threatened to engulf her. Then he jerked her forward into his arms, and their naked bodies collided.

'Sabbie…'

He began kissing her mouth, her throat and her breasts, his hands gliding over her flesh, bringing her alive.

Sabrina gulped at the air. She knew she ought to go back to her room. Knew they should have kept this marriage platonic. Because this could only end in disaster.

But she couldn't help herself.

Gently, she pushed him onto his back, kneeling beside him and kissing down his flat abdomen to linger between his thighs. He was hard now, fully aroused, and she bent to take him into her mouth.

'Yes,' he groaned, his head thrown back in ecstasy, eyes closed. *'Thee mou…*you enchantress.'

Being in charge for once was a revelation. The power and the lust, and yet the sweetness too…the sudden understanding of his need and vulnerability.

'Enough…' he groaned after a while.

Looking up through a curtain of hair, she caught the hot glint of his eyes as he gazed upon her nudity. He shifted beneath her, slowly positioning her so her thighs straddled his strong body, her wet core flush with his hips.

'Put me inside you,' he instructed, his face a taut

mask of need, and he groaned again as she complied, easing her core slowly down onto his broad crown. 'Yes, like that. Ah, that's good, *agape mou*.'

Cupping both breasts, he strummed his thumbs over her sensitive nipples until she whimpered, still straddling him. Then he thrust upwards, rocking her back and forth. She shook at his depth, her tenderness splayed wide, biting into her lower lip as her head tipped back, control fraying at the edges.

'Now, ride me.'

It was a command.

His hands gripped her hips, moving her in an age-old rhythm, teaching her how to ride his hard, muscular body until she shuddered and cried out. His breathing changed then, quickening. He rolled over, taking her with him, and thrust deep with a cry of triumph, on top of her now.

It felt so good. Sabrina lost all sense of time, gasping and kissing, raising her hips to meet his. Heat was pouring off them both in waves. He was hard as stone, his body like iron, and she was fluid, soft and flowing about him, wet and receptive.

She found herself mouthing the words *I love you...* over and over, but soft and soundless, under her breath so he couldn't hear. It was her secret, and she hugged it to herself even as mindless pleasure took her again...

In the depths of his nightmare Rafael had been a boy again, at home with his mother, holding her hand and soothing her tears with the comfort of his presence, which was all he'd had to give.

Then the door had crashed open and there was his father.

Papa.

Next thing, pleading and crying, he was being pushed into the tiny space under the floor where Papa hid his contraband whenever the police came calling. Terrified, bent double, Rafael had slammed his fists against the dusty wooden boards that held him captive, while above his head his father had removed his belt and beat his mother.

'No!' he kept shouting. 'Please stop it! Leave her alone.'

Then his eyes had opened to find Sabrina there, and the nightmare was over. Her passionate kisses had melted the dream into nothing, her sweet sex burning his fears away.

Now he heard her cry out, and his soul recognised the emotion in her voice, felt his skin catching fire along with hers.

Gasping to completion, he jerked and groaned, filling her with his seed, and found himself wishing she was not on the contraceptive pill. He had always sworn he would never have a child himself, fearing his own fitness to be a good parent, coming from a man like his father. But now he knew what he wanted. To conceive a child with this woman…to become a father and watch their baby grow…safe, nurtured and loved as he had never been…

* * *

Waking late the next morning, Rafael found himself alone in bed.

Feeling curiously hollow inside, he took a shower, dressed in blue jeans and a T-shirt, and went down to find Sabrina reading a novel by the pool.

'Good morning,' he said, feeling awkward, thrusting his hands in his jeans pockets.

He could still recall his nightmare, his desperate pleas to his father. She had admitted to hearing him cry out. How much had she heard last night before she'd come to his room?

She put down her book and looked up at him, sexy in skin-tight white shorts and a sky-blue midriff top that hugged her figure. Her gold-kissed skin glistened with sun oil. He couldn't decipher her expression, because large dark-framed sunglasses concealed her eyes. But her hands were clenched on the arms of the lounger, her body rigid.

'You had another nightmare,' she said, as though reading his mind.

'I remember.'

He drew up a lounger and sat beside her, watching the play of sunlight on the pool. His chest tightened as he moved his restless gaze over her gorgeous body, but he studiously avoided her face, afraid of what he might see there.

'I apologise. Did I frighten you?'

'No.' She put her novel aside. 'What was the dream about?'

'I don't want to discuss it.'

'You were shouting and moaning in your sleep,' she said softly, watching him. 'Something about your father? You sounded so desperate…so unhappy.'

He flushed, embarrassed by the thought of her witnessing his secret, long-buried pain. 'Flashback dream, my therapist calls them,' he admitted reluctantly.

'To the night your mother died?'

This was too close to the shame he kept hidden.

His jaw clenched hard. *You were shouting and moaning in your sleep.* She made him sound like a scared child…

'Yes,' he growled, and then, before she could mock him further, added in bitter self-loathing, 'And, yes, I *know* she died because I wasn't strong enough to protect her. You don't need to remind me.'

'What?' She stared at him, blinking.

'You always pretended you didn't know what had happened,' he ground out, unable to help himself. 'But everyone on Calista knew. It was all over the local paper.'

'Rafe, I genuinely have no idea what you're talking about. Your father murdered your mother and then shot himself. That's all I know. I certainly didn't read about it in the paper. I was barely ten at the time, remember?'

He gritted his teeth, struggling against the horrors of his past. But they refused to be suppressed any longer.

'My father often shoved me into a cubbyhole under the floor,' he burst out, 'the place where he hid stolen goods. It was his favourite punishment for me. But that night I had to listen as he beat my mother to death. I tried to get out of there, I swear. My hands were battered and bloody—' He broke off, and when he spoke again his voice was almost a howl. 'What kind of boy can't protect his own mother?'

There was horror in her face.

'You were only a child.' She shook her head, reaching out to him. 'There was nothing you could have done.'

'Mama trusted me. I let her down.'

'Hey, come here…'

Sabrina tried to hold him, but he jerked to his feet and turned away, his vision blurred with tears, unable to bear the thought of her pity.

'We've talked about this,' she continued gently. 'You can't blame yourself for what your father did. You were a victim too.'

'Is that the kind of man you want in your life, Sabbie? A victim?'

'You're not a victim any more—' she began, but he was no longer listening, struggling to hold onto his self-control.

'You went to bed in your own room last night.' His voice became clipped as he shifted topic to protect himself, busily tucking his painful past away, where it could no longer burst out and embarrass him. 'Is that how it's going to be from now on? Separate bedrooms?'

'You'd shut the door to your suite. I thought you didn't want me in there.'

'Not at all,' he said gruffly. 'I merely assumed you were tired after the Paris trip and needed time alone to sleep.' He thrust his hands into his pockets, glancing round at her. 'Talking of which…you left my bed in a hurry this morning. Couldn't wait to get away from me?'

He winced, falling silent. How needy that made him sound!

'Stop putting words in my mouth. Last night was… amazing.'

Amazing?

It had been incredible for him. But for her…?

She was being kind and comforting, of course. Because that was what friends did. Pain tore through him at the realisation that she saw him as vulnerable. Last night had revealed a terrible gaping hole at the centre of his being. He'd bared his past as he'd cried out like a frightened child in his sleep. He felt so ashamed, wishing she hadn't overheard his nightmare.

'But once you've left me,' he countered doggedly, trying to push his hurt and his fear deep down inside, where she couldn't see it, 'you won't waste any time thinking about me again. Just like when you left me behind at the orphanage. Out of sight, out of mind.'

'What the hell are you talking about, Rafe?'

She whipped off her sunglasses, glaring at him. Her eyes were red-rimmed, their lashes wet and stuck together. Had she been crying? The thought stunned him.

'I'm not planning on going anywhere. Besides, you're the one who forgot about *me*.'

'How do you work that out?'

'I wrote to you from London and never received a reply. In the end I just assumed you'd lost interest in me once I'd been adopted. And then in Paris—' Sabrina broke off and shook her head, her gaze dropping to the ground. 'Well, you certainly got your revenge that night.

You must have laughed yourself sick when you realised it was my first time…'

Her voice was choked. He was astonished. He thought at first this must be another elaborate ruse to disarm him. Then he looked into her eyes and wanted to weep too, seeing the hurt she was no longer bothering to hide.

'*Thee mou,*' he groaned, at once snapping out of his self-pity. 'Laugh at you? For being a virgin? *Never.* Though it was a surprise,' he admitted guiltily, digging his hands into his pockets. 'You told me you were on the pill.'

'For medical reasons. Reasons that still exist, in fact.' She looked embarrassed. 'I take the pill to regulate my periods.'

'I see.' He grimaced, feeling like a fool. 'But how could you ever think I would make love to you out of revenge?' he threw back at her. 'Revenge for what?'

'For being adopted and leaving you behind.' Her whisper was agonised.

'No, I was overjoyed that someone had finally seen your true worth. And such a man. A billionaire. I knew you would live in the lap of luxury, that your days of suffering were at an end. I was delighted for you, *kardia mou.*'

'So why didn't you write to me?' she wailed, tears streaming down her face.

'What?' His lungs felt as if they were packed with broken glass, every breath a torment. 'I *did* write to you.' He raked a hand through his hair. 'I wrote to you every month for the first year and got no reply.' He swallowed hard, recalling the bitter unhappiness of those days. 'In the end I stopped writing. I assumed you didn't want to know me any more.'

She was shaking her head. 'No… No, you didn't write. I didn't get any letters from you. Not a single one.'

A bewildered silence stretched between them.

Then Rafael groaned, slapping himself in the forehead. 'Templeton. I should have known. He must have intercepted my letters. Probably read them, tore them up and threw them in the bin.' Fury gnawed at his insides. 'That *bastard*.'

Her damp blue eyes were stretched wide. She put her hand to her throat, gripping herself as though she was having difficulty breathing. 'My father…? Surely he couldn't have…?' She bared her teeth. 'But of course he did. He tried to stop me writing to you that first year in England too. So I sneaked my letters out of the house instead.'

'I never got them.'

She was breathing heavily. 'The wardens at the orphanage… They were in his pocket too. And it worked. When you never replied, I gave up.' She let out a cry of despair. '*I gave up.* I let you down.'

'No, Sabrina, never…'

But she didn't seem to be listening. 'I loved the orphanage. I thought of it as my real home, even years after I'd been adopted. Now I can't see it the same way any more. It's all tainted.' Her throat convulsed. 'I should have let you knock it down.'

Inwardly, he cursed all the men who had caused her so much pain. Her father, the orphanage director, the wardens… But perhaps some good could come of that trauma.

'We could use the old orphanage as headquarters for our charity,' he suggested, following her as she walked away. 'Try to salvage something from this mess.'

There was a short silence. Slowly, she turned back to him. Her eyes were still swimming with tears. 'You still intend to go ahead with the charity?' Her voice was uncertain.

'Of course.' Rafael felt as if his heart was caught in a vice that was slowly tightening. 'Don't you want to work with me on that? To protect other orphans like ourselves?'

'Except I was never an orphan, was I? It was a lie. My father was still alive. I just didn't know it.'

Sabrina had stopped at the base of the steps up to the villa, her face half in sunlight, half in shadow. She looked so desolate it took his breath away.

'Marriage doesn't have to be a prison, Sabrina. It was for my mother, granted. But that's not what I want for us.'

Sabrina turned, came back to him. There was an odd look in her face. 'Then what *do* you want from our marriage, Rafe?' she asked softly.

He saw the trap too late.

Everything inside him was shaking. It was a seismic event in his soul. He could only control it by gritting his teeth and clenching his jaw. He wanted to reach for her, to kiss her fiercely and fold her in his arms for ever. To show her that they belonged to each other and always had.

But he knew she would push him away… Sooner or later she would see through his brash over-confidence to the weakness at his heart. Because he *must* be weak, mustn't he? Otherwise he would not have failed his own mother when she'd needed him most.

'For us to be friends,' he mumbled, not meeting her eyes. 'Soulmates.'

'And lovers?' she whispered, and she took his hand before he could snatch it away. 'For us to love each other, Rafe?'

The old familiar darkness gripped his heart and began to spread, tightening its stranglehold on his throat, his larynx.

'That's not possible,' he told her between numb lips. 'I'm not capable of love. It's not in my nature.'

'Everyone is capable of love.'

'Not me.' His smile was a grimace, showing his teeth. 'I don't deserve love. I've never done anything in my life to deserve a happy ending.'

'You've been my friend,' she pointed out unsteadily, her blue eyes glistening with tears he longed to kiss away. 'You've helped me escape my father…to see him for what he is.'

'That took no special skill. Only the truth.'

'And the orphans. You've helped them.'

'I only did what was necessary to hook you in,' he lied, hoping to make her hate him, because that would make everything easier. 'So I could get those US negotiations done. Make more money.'

'I don't believe you. And you *do* deserve love,' she insisted. 'We both do.'

But the tears were spilling down her cheeks now. She looked unhappier than ever, and Rafael knew with a plummeting heart that it was his fault. He had done this by marrying her. He had made Sabrina miserable, just as his father had made his mother miserable. And now they were locked in a spiralling fall from which only divorce could free them.

'No…' he croaked, as bitterness at his own failure flooded him. Everything inside him was hot and painful. 'Please don't cry,' he said hoarsely. 'I'm sorry if you misunderstood my motives. I didn't marry you in search of some fairy-tale ending, Sabbie. I married you because…'

He stopped, unable to say the words that would reveal his weakness. Because he knew how tender-hearted she could be, and he didn't want any decision she made about their marriage to be based on pity for an old friend. That would be unbearable.

'Well, none of that matters now. I guess we've both achieved our goals. So if you want that divorce straight away, I won't contest it.' His heart winced in agony, and it was all he could do not to cry out and beg her to stay. 'I can instruct my lawyers today. Just say the word.'

It wasn't what he wanted, but he couldn't bear the thought of her being locked into the misery and suffering of an unhappy marriage as his mother had been.

Clenching a fist against her mouth, Sabrina stared at him wide-eyed in silence—and then she stilled, looking up. A helicopter was approaching fast, a flash of silver in the azure sky. And multiple vehicles too. Rafael could hear the repeated bump of heavy tyres over the uneven track that led to the villa and he frowned.

More paparazzi?

Except he'd instructed the perimeter guards to keep all members of the press away from their home. So who the hell had let them through?

CHAPTER TWELVE

SABRINA STARED AT Rafael in consternation. Not because of the incoming helicopter—though she guessed from his frown that it meant trouble—but because it seemed their short marriage was over sooner than planned. Already he was talking of divorce.

In Paris, she had briefly dared to hope again, especially when he'd floated the idea of the charity for orphans… But she knew in her heart that even those few sweet hours together in the city of love had changed nothing. Sooner or later Rafael would walk away again, exactly as he'd done five years ago, proving her own worst fears correct.

The helicopter was landing. They heard feet on the steps down to the pool and then Kyria Diakou appeared on the veranda, looking embarrassed.

'Apologies, sir, madam!' the housekeeper called down to them breathlessly. 'But there are men at the door. One claims to be a lawyer and another is a police officer. They say you are keeping Kyria Romano here against her will and her father is coming to take her home.' She looked flustered. 'What should I do?'

Rafael said nothing but looked at Sabrina, his face a stony mask.

'I'll speak to them.' Sabrina swept up the steps to the house without a backward look at her husband. 'It's time I put a stop to this nonsense.'

She was heartily sick of men treating her like a chattel, telling her what to think and how to live her life and always expecting her to obey.

When she threw open the front entrance door she found her father waiting impatiently on the other side of it. Behind him stood a small army of bodyguards, some men in suits, whom she presumed to be part of his vast legal team, and a police officer in Calistan uniform, looking uncomfortable.

'Dearest!' Andrew Templeton exclaimed, and embraced her before she could say a word. 'I'm relieved to see you looking so well. Now, listen…don't worry about this marriage to Romano. I can get you out of it in five minutes flat—just leave everything to me.'

She had too much pride to make a scene in front of an audience.

'You'd better come in, Dad,' was all she replied, speaking as calmly as she could manage while seething with emotion.

As soon as he'd stepped through the door, she closed it in the face of his entourage, ignoring their loud protests.

'But only you, and only for five minutes. Then you need to leave.'

'More games, Sabrina?'

Her father dominated the hallway, moving restlessly

to examine the statues on display, his hat in his hand. Now she knew the truth about her parentage she could clearly see the features she'd inherited from him. The sculpted cheekbones, the wiry build, even the blond hair—though his was silvery now. At least she had her mother's blue eyes…

Her heart ached as she remembered the mother she'd lost, and she wished Cherie could have told her the truth.

'I'm not leaving Calista without you.' He turned to face her, hard authority in his voice. 'Pack your bags. My lawyers are here to serve annulment papers on Rafael Romano. Then I'm taking you home to London.'

Sabrina drew in a deep breath. 'No, you're not.'

'Why? Is there something else we need to clear up before you can leave?'

He looked impatiently about the villa, his polished shoes and severe dark suit and tie out of place in these relaxed surroundings.

'The clock is ticking, Sabrina. I need to get back in the air as soon as possible.' He grimaced. 'I've always hated this island.'

'Is that because you met my mother here?'

Her father turned to stare, arrested. 'Your *mother*? What on earth are you talking about?'

'You got my text, so don't pretend.'

'Your text?' He pulled out his mobile and nimbly flicked through the screens. 'You mean this nonsense about knowing who I am?'

'I know *everything*, Dad,' she told him, forestalling any attempt he might have made to keep lying. 'How you abandoned Cherie when she told you she was pregnant, and how you made the decision not to claim me after she died.'

She had thought she had herself under control, but her voice was shaking.

'How you left me to rot in that orphanage for years, and then swept in like a knight on a white charger to adopt me... All the while knowing you were my *actual* biological father.' She shook her head when he opened his mouth to deny it, adding sharply, 'No, don't waste your breath. I've got a dossier of evidence to prove it.'

Andrew Templeton blinked, taken aback by this direct attack. For once, he seemed lost for words.

'So you can forget about rescuing me from Rafael,' she went on raggedly, 'because you're the one who's leaving Calista—not me.' She thrust her chin in the air to meet his stunned expression. 'And take your minions with you. They're not welcome here, and neither are you.'

'Sabrina...'

Her father took a step towards her but halted at her protest. A look of sly calculation came over his face.

'Okay, I can see how this might look bad,' he backtracked slowly. 'But I...I was in love with your mother. That's the honest truth.' He ran a hand through his thinning hair, his mouth compressed. 'It was just...I loved my wife more.'

There was a hint of despair in his voice—just enough to be believable.

'Cherie understood my dilemma. She never complained, so long as I took care of the two of you financially. I certainly didn't force that choice on her. You have to believe me.' He grimaced. 'She was born in England—I expect she told you that?'

When Sabrina nodded, he added, 'She left because of some trouble with the police. Some minor theft. She would have risked prison if she'd returned. That's why she was happy to stay on Calista with you...away from her past.' He shrugged. 'I helped that happen.'

That was news to her, and she wished her mother could have shared it with her. But it did make sense, at least.

'And after my mother died?' she asked.

He grimaced. 'I couldn't risk telling Barbara about the affair. Admit that I'd had a daughter by another woman. She would have left me.'

'So you threw me to the wolves instead.'

'Don't be so melodramatic.'

His brows tugged together in a look she knew well.

'I made sure you were well cared for. I paid the orphanage director a small fortune over the years to ensure it, and received regular updates on your health and progress. I did consider owning up... Only then Barbara got sick, and I couldn't hurt her like that when she was dying. After she passed away I flew straight out here to find you and take you back to England with me. Hardly *throwing you to the wolves*, is it?'

Andrew Templeton held out a hand, his look one of entreaty now. 'Come home and we can sort this mess out.'

She shook her head, hurt beyond measure to hear his candid confession. 'None of that explains why you "adopted" me…why you didn't admit who I was as soon as you'd taken me to England.'

'I couldn't have done that to your siblings. Tom and Pippa would have been devastated. They'd have hated me for betraying their mother, and would have found a way to blame you too.'

Sabrina could readily believe that, given how privileged her brother and sister were, and how they'd always looked down on her as an outsider to the family.

'But I've never begrudged you anything, have I?' her father went on. 'Since bringing you to live with me, I've given you the best education, clothes, jewellery, business opportunities… Because you're my daughter and I love you.'

'Is that why you refused treatment for my facial scars while I was in the orphanage? And told the director I wasn't to be adopted? Or why you hid Rafael's letters from me?' Pain wrenched at her. 'You let me think my closest friend had forgotten about me.'

'Barbara's cancer was terminal by the time the orphanage director approached me about facial surgery,' he told her, seeming unabashed by her accusations. 'I knew she didn't have long to live, and I wanted to wait until I could bring you home and get you the finest surgeons. As for that boy's letters… You were only a kid, for God's sake. I did it all for the best.'

'You did it for *yourself*,' she countered angrily. 'But you failed. Rafael and I still found each other again.'

'*"Found each other"?'* His lips twisted in a sneer. 'Do you know why Romano actually married you? For money. No other reason. He could have clicked his fingers and married any woman he likes. But he chose you.' He shook his head contemptuously. 'Romano found out I'm your real father and smelt a potential lawsuit. He knows you'll be a fabulously wealthy woman one day and he wants to jump on the gravy train.'

'He's already a billionaire, Dad.'

'You naïve little idiot.' He laughed harshly. 'A man can never have too much money. Have you learned nothing from living with me?' He cleared his throat, and that look of calculation was back in his face as he added, 'You can tell Romano I'm prepared to settle out of court if he agrees to keep this quiet.'

'I've heard enough.'

Sickened, Sabrina opened the front door. His men surged forward, trying to push past her. She held up a hand, announcing loudly in English, 'My father is leaving.' She turned to address the police officer in Greek. 'I'm sorry you've had a wasted trip. But my husband and I are on our honeymoon and would prefer not to be disturbed again.'

The police officer smiled politely. 'In that case, Kyria Romano, please accept my apologies and enjoy the rest of your honeymoon,' he said, and headed back to the gate.

The others fell back in his wake, confused, and her father had little choice but to leave the villa, gesturing for his men to return to their vehicles too.

'Goodbye, Dad,' she said coldly.

Andrew Templeton stepped into deep sunshine, a frown in his eyes. 'You're making a big mistake,' he warned her, resettling his hat on his silvery hair. 'I've had your husband investigated. I know all about his sordid affairs. He'll never stay faithful to you.'

Closing the door on her father, Sabrina stood with her head bowed, her whole body shaking. From beyond the villa walls she heard the sound of rotor blades whirring, louder and louder, and the steady retreat of vehicles along the dirt tracks of Calista.

She waited, expecting Rafael to appear, demanding to know what had been said.

But he didn't come.

Tears streamed down her face and she dashed them away. Of course he hadn't come to speak to her after her father left. He didn't care. He hadn't married her for some 'fairy-tale ending', as he'd said. It had all been strictly business.

'He'll never stay faithful to you.'

She bent over, sobbing silently, stifling the sound against her hand. Once again she was all alone in the world, with nobody to turn to for love and support.

Thea found her weeping and drew her gently into the lounge. 'Let me fetch you something cool to drink,' the housekeeper insisted, her eyes concerned, and bustled away to return with a glass of sharp-tasting home-made lemonade. 'This will help you feel better, *kyria*. It's the heat, that's all.'

But they both knew she was lying.

Feeling as if she'd been hit by a truck, Sabrina sipped the lemonade and then curled up on the couch, only meaning to close her eyes for a moment. But her body was exhausted...

She woke with a start some time later, catching the

sound of someone saying her name. The Diakous were arguing softly in the hallway.

Groggily, she wandered out. 'What's the matter? I fell asleep.'

Thea turned to her, her kindly face creased in lines of anxiety. 'Oh, *kyria*, I apologise for disturbing you. We can't seem to find Kyrios Romano.'

'What do you mean?'

'I saw your husband leave the villa by the side door when your father arrived,' Nikos explained hesitantly. 'We don't know where he went. But he's taken the sports car.' His bushy brows tugged together in concern. 'I saw his face when he was leaving… He was so unhappy, *kyria*. I've never seen him look like that.'

Cold fear gripped Sabrina's heart. 'Like what?'

'Like he might do himself a mischief,' the man said bluntly, ignoring his wife's protest.

Sabrina felt a hollowness inside. Her skin cooled, her chest tight with dread. She ought to have gone to find Rafael as soon as her father had gone. Though perhaps he'd already left the villa by then. But she'd been in pieces…unable to breathe properly, let alone explain what had passed between her and her father.

Rafael had claimed he didn't deserve love. That he wasn't even capable of it himself. Her heart had broken to hear him say such things. But she didn't believe any of that. It was merely his past talking—his memory of a beloved mother lost to a violent bully he hadn't been able to defeat.

Guilt flooded her—and a hot tide of remorse. They'd always stood up for each other in the orphanage, pushing

back against the bullies and the haters. In her scramble
to escape what she'd seen as the trap of their marriage
she'd forgotten the most essential thing that bound them
together. They were soulmates.

'I think I know where he may have gone,' she said.
'But I'll need a lift.'

'At once, *kyria*,' Nikos agreed, beaming.

Eyes shut tight, Rafael drew his knees to his chin and
hugged them. Dust settled about him in the silence of
the old orphanage. As soon as he'd heard Sabrina invite
Templeton inside he'd gone to listen, to be sure her father wasn't going to bully her, and prepared to leap to
his wife's defence if necessary. But once she'd so bravely
sent him packing Rafael had also left the villa, unseen
via the side door.

He'd needed time alone to think.

He was proud of his wife. So fiercely proud he thought
his heart would burst. The way she had handled her arrogant, overbearing father... Yet, despite her stubborn
denials to her dad, he knew their marriage was still over.
And deservedly so.

He couldn't give Sabrina love because he couldn't
accept love in return.

*'If you want that divorce straight away, I won't con-
test it. I can instruct my lawyers today. Just say the
word.'*

Their discussion had been interrupted by Templeton's arrival. But of *course* she would choose to divorce
him. There was no doubt in his mind. Why would such

a courageous, free-spirited woman, given the chance to escape, want to remain with a man as damaged as him?

This dark, cramped space was where Sabrina had hidden from the bullies as a child. Now he was hiding here too—but from himself. If he'd been a stronger person... if he'd spoken what was in his heart instead of fearing the darkness inside...perhaps he would have deserved her as a wife. Now he was going to lose her.

She had pointed out his appalling behaviour in Paris, how he'd so cruelly walked away after taking her virginity. An unforgivable act. Only he hadn't walked away. In truth, he'd run, and kept on running for years. Terrified by the sheer, fathomless depth of his love for her and his unfitness to share her life...

Rafael groaned, tugging violently on his hair. Sabrina didn't need him. She didn't need anyone and had just proved that. Besides, what did he know about love? He had made his fortune, become the infamous Rafael Romano, simply in order to impress her from afar. To prove he was more than the broken boy she'd known before—that he was somebody worth loving.

But the truth was, he was unlovable.

Looking to the future had always been one of his favourite ways to plan his next move. Yet all he could see ahead was loneliness. No woman except Sabrina had ever meant anything to him. Now she was going to leave him his life would be cold and barren. Barely worth living...

He heard a door thud and footsteps approaching his hiding place.

A memory rose up from the dark to scourge him, and he tensed, shaking his head. 'No!' he cried.

In his mind's eye Rafael saw his father tear open the cubbyhole under the floorboards, a long hairy arm reaching in to grab him and drag him out for another vicious beating.

He shrank back. 'I won't let you touch me!' He yelled into the void, down the turbulent spiral of years. 'Never again. You'll never touch me again, do you hear?'

Then the cupboard door was opening, dusty light pouring in, and he saw Sabrina crouched there, blue eyes wide with concern, golden hair spilling over her shoulders, exactly like the princess in a fairy story he had always known her to be.

'Okay,' she said huskily, and reached in to take his hand. 'Though for what it's worth, that would be a shame.'

Sabrina had guessed instinctively where he would be, knowing where *she* would have gone if it had felt like the end. Somewhere quiet and remote…somewhere she could retreat from the cruelties of the world.

On arrival at the old orphanage she'd spotted Rafael's sports car, drawn up outside, and told Nikos to go back to Villa Rosa without her.

'I'll come back later with my husband,' she'd assured him.

And sure enough she had found Rafael hiding there, and known it was fate. They were still soulmates, able to read each other's thoughts. All she needed now was to hear him say aloud what he was truly thinking and feeling, without trying to conceal it. Because without that it would all be pointless.

Together, they wandered out of the empty orphanage and stood in the fragrant silence, looking up at the crumbling, flower-bright façade.

'I'm sorry I walked out on you again,' he said gruffly.

'There's nothing to apologise for.'

'I listened to you and Templeton… I hope you don't mind. I heard you tell him to leave.' There was a grim smile on his face. 'I was so proud of you.'

'Thank you.' She expelled a long breath. 'Yes, that whole disgraceful charade is over. I made sure my father understood. Now I just have to decide what to do with that information.'

It was going to be a difficult few years, she thought. But she would get through it, with or without Rafael. She had found her strength now, and knew she didn't need anyone to hold her hand through this new phase of her life.

Though it would be nice not to do it alone…

She stared up into the blue Calistan sky, remembering their unconventional childhood here, the crazy dreams they had whispered to each other when no one else was listening.

'Are you going to ask me for a divorce?' Rafael's voice was bleak.

She took a deep breath and weighed up her options. 'Only if you don't tell me the truth, Rafe,' she said bluntly.

He flinched. 'The truth?'

'About why you left me in Paris after the first time we slept together.'

A muscle jerked in his cheek as he considered that. 'I left because I was terrified,' he said at last, as if the words had been drawn from him grudgingly.

'Terrified?' She stared at him in disbelief.

He looked away, grimacing. 'I couldn't get out of your hotel room fast enough. I was utterly mesmerised by you, Sabbie. I'd never wanted a woman so much in my life. And suddenly we were in bed together. And it was perfect. Better than perfect...it was miraculous.' He sucked in an unsteady breath before adding, 'I know you didn't see, but I...I cried while we were making love.'

She felt her own eyes water at this startling admission, and a hollow ache in her chest. 'You *cried*?'

'I couldn't help it,' he grated, jaw clenched, looking for all the world like a man in front of a firing squad. 'Next morning, I looked at you and knew why.' There was a red tint along his cheekbones. 'Because I was head over heels in love with you.'

She gasped, hardly daring to believe it. 'In *love* with me? You?' Sweet joy flooded her as he nodded. 'This, from the man who claims he can't love anyone?'

'I had to say something,' he mumbled stiffly. 'To stop you suspecting.'

'Oh, Rafe...' She touched his stubbled cheek, wishing he wasn't such an idiot. 'But if that's how you felt, why hurt me by walking out? Why not just tell me?'

'I'm sorry. I didn't want to hurt you.' He was struggling, his eyes darkening. 'But I couldn't run the risk of losing you. Don't you see? I knew I wouldn't be able to keep you and it would all end in disaster. I didn't deserve you, and I had nothing to offer you. I mean, you already had everything you could possibly want.'

Except love, she thought, but said nothing, watching him in hope.

'The fear was intense… It was like watching a meteor approaching. The end of everything.' He ran a hand across his eyes. 'So I got up and ran—like the coward I am.'

Her heart broke for him. 'You're no coward. The things you've done…the way you've risen above your past… All that took incredible courage and determination. And as for not deserving me—'

'Oh, I know all that. But deep inside,' he said hoarsely, jabbing at his chest, 'I still feel the guilt of my mother's death.' He looked at her, his expression poignant. 'I should be able to protect the woman I love.'

'I don't need protecting,' she assured him.

'But your father… I should have gone to meet him and knocked him down before he even reached the villa. Not let him anywhere near you.'

'It was my business and I sent him away on my own,' she reminded him. 'All I need from you is love, Rafe.' She swallowed at the magnitude of those words, her stomach full of butterflies. 'If you still have feelings for me, that is.'

'Are you kidding?'

He kissed her on the lips and the world spun.

When he spoke again his voice was gruff, uneven with emotion. 'I love you so much, Sabbie. More than words.'

'I love you too, Rafe.'

They clung together for a few miraculous minutes, just letting those words sink into the air between them.

'It's stupid, but for a long while after Paris I truly thought you'd only wanted me for this.' She touched her unscarred face. 'And that once you were bored, you'd leave me again. I always seem to lose what I love…'

'Your mother?' he asked, narrow-eyed.

She nodded, trembling as she remembered that first traumatic loss.

'I will never, ever get *bored*, as you put it, and I will never leave you. This is for ever. I know it the way I know my own name.' He laid his warm cheek against hers, whispering, 'That first time with you in Paris I lost control. I'd never cried in bed with a woman before and it blew my mind. That was when I realised you were the one, for sure. But I also knew that if I admitted how I felt and you *rejected* me I would be broken. I could never be whole again.'

'I'm not going to reject you, Rafael Romano,' she promised him, raising her head to look him in the eye. 'I'm going to love you until you can't stand.'

His mouth quirked. 'That sounds…acceptable.'

Sabrina glanced at the sun-drenched building behind them. At last its old walls seemed beloved to her again. The taint of her father's lies was gone for ever, and this new joy was blotting out the past.

'Is this what you intended when you bought the orphanage?' she asked him. 'To bring us back together?'

'Not consciously. But the heart wants what the heart wants…'

She gave a gasp of laughter, a lightness inside her

that she hadn't known in years. Not since she'd been a little girl. 'This must be what happiness feels like,' she said wonderingly.

'Yes,' he agreed, his gaze arrowing down to her mouth. 'That,' he murmured, 'and this.'

And he kissed her.

EPILOGUE

Two years later

'THERE IT IS!' Rafael called above the noise of the rotor blades as Villa Rosa came into view of the helicopter.

It was mid-afternoon and the walls were bathed in golden light. The Aegean sparkled beyond them in a deep blue dream of summer.

'Are you glad to be back on the island at last?' Sabrina asked her daughter.

Now a shy thirteen-year-old, Cora had been their daughter for nearly a year, adopted from the Calistan orphanage to come and live with them in New York.

Now they were all coming home to Villa Rosa for a few weeks of relaxation.

'Of course,' Cora told them both eagerly, plaiting her shoulder-length dark hair. 'I can't wait to see all my old friends at the orphanage.'

She had kept in touch with the other orphans, and always gave little shrieks of joy whenever one of them found new parents.

'But I love New York too,' she added with an impish smile. 'All those bookshops… I could never have too many books.'

'Our little bookworm,' Rafael said, and there was warm pride in his voice.

Sabrina grinned approvingly.

As soon as the helicopter touched down they shepherded Cora towards Villa Rosa, where the Diakous stood waiting to welcome them, their faces wreathed in smiles.

'It's so hot… Can I jump in the pool straight away?' Cora pleaded.

'Give us ten minutes, then we'll all swim together,' Sabrina told her, watching happily as the girl dashed upstairs, her heavy rucksack bouncing on her back, full of paperbacks to be read over the holiday.

She and Rafael followed more slowly, heading for the master bedroom. It had been a long flight and she was jet lagged. But it was so lovely to be back on Calista.

Her heart swelled with joy as she took in the familiar views, and the sun glinting on water far below the cliffs. The bedroom had been redecorated in seablue, with fresh flowers arranged in every alcove and thick fleece rugs under their feet, and it welcomed them home. And the crystal dolphin Rafael had bought her as a wedding gift stood on display beside the vast bed, reminding them both of the origins of their love story.

Rafael put down the bag he'd been carrying and took her in his arms. 'It's good to be home.'

They kissed deeply, and Sabrina felt her bones turn to water. 'Not now,' she whispered, laughing. 'Cora is waiting to swim.'

'Of course.' His dark eyes glowed. 'But after she's

gone to bed this evening, what do you say to a late candlelit dinner for two on the veranda? Just like our first night here.'

'I'd love that.' Sabrina sank her teeth deep into her lower lip and caught his arm as he turned away. 'Wait… There's something I need to tell you.'

Rafael readily came back into her arms, stroking his hands down her spine, his intense gaze meeting hers. 'I'm all ears, my love.'

'And all hands too!' she exclaimed.

'I can't help it. Not with the way you're beginning to round out these days.' He caught her quick look and said hurriedly, 'Don't get me wrong. I love it. You look incredibly sexy.'

Sabrina blushed. It was time to tell him what she'd discovered only that morning. Especially since he was about to see her squeeze into a bikini for the first time in ages.

'Rafael, I know you said we'd wait until Cora was more settled, but it seems Nature had other ideas…' Seeing his stare, she added nervously, 'I'm pregnant.'

He stilled, his gaze dropping to the soft swell of her belly. 'We're having a baby?'

He gave a whoop of joy and spun her around, lifting her feet off the ground.

'*Kardia mou,*' he whispered against her cheek, his voice hoarse with emotion. 'You make me the happiest of men…' His gaze raked her face. 'You're happy too? This is what you want?'

'I've never been happier.' Tears of joy squeezed from under Sabrina's eyelids. 'I just hope Cora won't mind a little brother or sister. We'll love both our children equally.'

'Both equally,' Rafael agreed, and leant forward,

breathing in her scent. 'Is it wrong that I have the craziest urge to make mad, passionate love to you?'

'Yes, very wrong.' She laughed at his frustrated expression. 'Later, darling, after that candlelit dinner. Then we can play at being newlyweds again.'

After changing for the pool, they went downstairs together to join Cora.

'Linda rang during the flight, by the way,' he told Sabrina softly. 'She says we're all set for the big launch next month.'

'That's wonderful.'

They'd set up their charity supporting orphans worldwide, and had been busy acquiring premises in major cities.

'We're still keeping Calista as our official headquarters, though?'

Rafael nodded. 'Tomorrow we'll take the helicopter to the old orphanage and see how the refurb is progressing.' He smiled at her excitement. 'Your vision is coming true, Sabrina.'

'I couldn't have done it without you,' she said, waving to Cora as they descended through the hot fragrant sunshine to the poolside. 'If you hadn't agreed not to demolish the orphanage, none of this would be happening.'

'And if you hadn't come to find me that day—'

'I will *always* find you,' she told him, stopping to kiss him on the lips. 'It's fate, Rafe. We were meant to be together.'

* * * * *

Did you get lost in the fantasy of
Her Convenient Vow to the Billionaire?

Then be sure to watch out for
Jane Holland's next story
from Harlequin Presents!

#4137 NINE MONTHS TO SAVE THEIR MARRIAGE
by Annie West

After his business-deal wife leaves, Jack is intent on getting their on-paper union back on track. He just never imagined their reunion would be *scorching*. Or that their red-hot Caribbean nights would leave Bess *pregnant*! Is this their chance to finally find happiness?

#4138 PREGNANT WITH HER ROYAL BOSS'S BABY
Three Ruthless Kings
by Jackie Ashenden

King Augustine may rule a kingdom, but loyal assistant Freddie runs his calendar. There's no task she can't handle. Except perhaps having to tell her boss she's going to need some time off...because in six months she'll be having *his* heir!

#4139 THE SPANIARD'S LAST-MINUTE WIFE
Innocent Stolen Brides
by Caitlin Crews

Sneaking into ruthless Spaniard Lionel's wedding ceremony, Geraldine arrives just in time to see him being jilted. But Lionel is still in need of a convenient wife...and innocent Geraldine suddenly finds *herself* being led to the altar!

#4140 A VIRGIN FOR THE DESERT KING
The Royal Desert Legacy
by Maisey Yates

After years spent as a political prisoner, Sheikh Riyaz has been released. Now it's Brianna's job to prepare him for his long-arranged royal wedding. But the forbidden attraction flaming between them tempts her to cast duty—and her *innocence*!—to the desert winds...

HPCNMRA0823

#4141 REDEEMED BY MY FORBIDDEN HOUSEKEEPER
by Heidi Rice

Recovering from a near-deadly accident, playboy Renzo retreated to his Côte d'Azur estate. Nothing breaks through his solitude. Until the arrival of his new yet strangely familiar housekeeper, Jessie, stirs dormant desires...

#4142 HIS JET-SET NIGHTS WITH THE INNOCENT
by Pippa Roscoe

When archaeologist Evelyn needs his help saving her professional reputation, Mateo reluctantly agrees. Only the billionaire hadn't bargained on a quest around the world... From Spain to Shanghai, each city holds a different adventure. Yet one thing is constant: their intoxicating attraction!

#4143 HOW THE ITALIAN CLAIMED HER
by Jennifer Hayward

To save his failing fashion house, CEO Cristiano needs the face of the brand, Jensen, to clean up her headline-hitting reputation. But while she's lying low at his Lake Como estate, he's caught between his company...and his desire for the scandalous supermodel!

#4144 AN HEIR FOR THE VENGEFUL BILLIONAIRE
by Rosie Maxwell

Memories of his passion-fueled night with Carrie consume tycoon Damon. Until he discovers the ugly past that connects them and pledges to erase every memory of her. Then she storms into his office...and announces she's carrying his child!

YOU CAN FIND MORE INFORMATION ON UPCOMING HARLEQUIN TITLES, FREE EXCERPTS AND MORE AT HARLEQUIN.COM.

HPCNMRB0823

HARLEQUIN
PLUS

Try the best multimedia
subscription service for romance
readers like you!

Read, Watch and Play.

Experience the easiest way to get
the romance content you crave.

Start your **FREE TRIAL** at
<u>www.harlequinplus.com/freetrial</u>.